An Embarrassment of Riches

Michael Kuiack

Illustrations by Daryl Stephenson

Clockwork Books

Dedicated to
Adam and Simon and Leah

Without me there is no you.
Without you there is no me.

They say of an amputee that he remembers his leg. Well, I remember this girl. I am not whole without her. I am not alive without her. When she was with me I was more alive than I have ever been, and not only when she was pleasant either. Even when we were fighting I was whole. At the time I didn't realize how important it was, but I do now. I am not a dope. I know that if I should win her I'll have many horrible times. Over and over, I'll wish I'd never seen her. But I also know that if I fail I'll never be a whole man. I'll live a gray half-life, and I'll mourn for my lost girl every hour of the rest of my life. As thoughtful reptiles you will wonder, 'Why not wait? Look further! There are better fish in the sea!' But you are not involved. Let me tell you that to me not only are there no better fish, there are no other fish in the sea at all. The sea is lonely without this fish.

John Steinbeck – Sweet Thursday

An Embarrassment of Riches

"Mr. Edgars."

I swivelled my head slightly, slowly, to the left, keeping my eyes down toward the floor. The day was very early and very bright. I was sitting on the scuffed hardwood floor of our common living room in front of the stereo, listening to the Gandharvas very loud. They were my latest hangover remedy, the Gandharvas were. Loud, with lots of coffee with lots of cream and sugar for energy and eventually something light to eat and I would be ready to face another day. This morning, that prognosis seemed optimistic, even unlikely. I thought I might be terminal. A thousand-dollar tip from Mr. Stevenson's table the night before had been my undoing. He was some kind of a sand and gravel and concrete magnate, the owner of several mammoth pits dotted irregularly around the outskirts of our little town and a noisy plant down by the river where it turned the corner and disappeared from sight. His name was emblazoned on dozens of trucks. He was a loud boor of a man desperate to appear cultured in the eyes of his new younger-model wife and her stylish friends. I could read him like a book. In for dinner then off to the theatre to see a play that not a one of them would understand and back for late drinks and snacks, $3,900 worth all told and let's make it an even $5,000 shall we, Doug? I had said absolutely, Mr. Stevenson, done like dinner. I kissed his ass and I fetched and I scraped and I flirted with his too young, too blonde wife until he and his guests and colleagues were all pickled enough to run off to their beds with their respective concrete wives.

For my part, I had taken the spoils straight to Bentley's arriving in plenty of time for last call. I had a few belts there and a couple of lines in the ladies room and then the booze can and then somebody's house and some smoke before the cab ride home. I had collapsed in my bed still in my not-so-starched-anymore white shirt and tuxedo pants to be up late for the Gandharvas and lots of coffee with lots of cream and sugar for energy and eventually something light to eat and I would be ready to face another day. Not a bad night's work and, for me, just one of too many in a long series, the start of which I could barely remember.

*

"Doug."

Again.

My name again.

This time the voice was clearly that of Christa, one of my house-mates, that much I knew. Christa was a waitress at The Abbey, the best, most expensive restaurant in town. She wore fishnets and a push-up bra and a little black dress at work and raked it in. She had been wearing tiny, pink panties and a longish T-shirt when I had stumbled down from my room that morning. Looking delectable as always, puffy nipples out to there, the cheeks of her bum half-moons, edible but lesbian through and through. More's the pity. I assumed she was still dressed much the same. I could see one of her feet and part of one long, bare leg just at the edge of my peripheral vision. She had nicked herself shaving. There was a brown-y bruise on one knee. Her toe nails needed doing and I surmised she was going through one of her 'who gives a shit', somewhere between relationships stage. I knew that stage well.

"Doug, these guys are here for you."

Her voice was louder now, insistent even. She put the accent on the 'you' in the sentence as if she needed to draw my attention to the strangeness of the situation. No one ever came to see me at the house, certainly not in the morning, certainly not on a Sunday. She was even sounding a little alarmed and that alarm began its work on me.

*

I swivelled my head slightly, slowly, further to the left.

I saw a pair of trousers, blue wool or maybe flannel, expensive, certainly too heavy for the weather lately. Left a little further, carefully, and up into jacket matching pants and further up, carefully, to the face of a patrician, grey-headed man, looking much like a character from some soap opera, the dying denizen of the failing family business perhaps. Not a villain. More like a sneak.

"Blake Carrington," I thought. "I'm being visited by Blake Carrington. I'm being visited by Blake Carrington because I snorted too much coke last night and acted the fool at Bentley's."

"Mr. Edgars."

This time from another voice, too far right of the center of the back of my head to register visually.

"Douglas Edgars! Are you Mr. Douglas Edgars?"

The different voice again. Irritated. Insistent. Much too loud for the circumstances. A voice used to being listened to and right quick; a finger snapper surely and a lousy tipper.

I turned. My head still was not quite right, still feeling too light and all floaty with a dull, little pain in the front like from a long-buried bullet.

"Yes."

I muttered my agreement, not entirely sure that this scene was happening at all but willing to go with it until it worked itself into something different or better, something I could handle; a passing thought perhaps, a fancy, even better, a dream.

"Do you have any identification at all, Sir?"

I looked at Blake for what seemed a very long time. He and his co-star had me at a disadvantage. I was still seated. They were standing in the clouds. The Gandharvas played on around us, very loud.

"Not on me," I said, looking down past my naked

chest at my sweats. I could smell my own miserable, beery sweat.

"We will need to see some identification, please, before we proceed." The other one spoke again.

They were so much the same they could have been two halves of the same person but they were standing just far enough apart that there had to be two of them.

"Who are you? The police?"

I searched my mind for fresh crimes and came up blank.

"We're lawyers, Mr. Edgar," the younger, louder one said. "We have important matters to discuss with you, most important matters, legal matters. (He enunciated 'legal' like it was the name of God.) Could we see some identification?"

He paused as if that speech was enough to answer any questions I might have and assuage my guilt over past misdeeds and forgive even those I didn't remember. They were both gazing at me more directly than was comfortable. My intuition had deserted me. I had no idea what they were thinking. I had no idea if I was thinking at all. Like an automaton, I acquiesced in the face of authority, nodded, stood, and headed upstairs to grab my wallet and a tee-shirt. I came downstairs holding my driver's license in front of me like a Get Out of Jail Free card.

The Gandharvas played on in the background.

Very loud.

*

"What do you guys want," I asked?

My voice sounded funny to me. Too loud. Too high. Different. I moved to turn down the music.

Both suits ignored my question. One suit – navy blue flannel I had decided – had taken my license and examined it carefully, both sides, then both sides again as if admiring the quality work of the counterfeiter, before handing it over to the other suit – jet black wool with a subtle pinstripe. Again, both sides and again. They exchanged a glance around and beyond me and the first one pulled out a card and handed it over as if it would answer all my questions. It didn't.

Carefully, I read;

Jerome Carruthers
Attorney at Law
Some address in San Francisco.

I was beginning to hit my stride. The coffee, the cream and sugar, being upright for a while, the brisk walk up and down the stairs, their evident discomfort, the very strangeness of them co-existing in a world with me, had all worked to give me some strength. Holding the one card in my left hand, running my thumb over the raised lettering, fingering the thick bond, thinking these guys are expensive, I looked at the second suit and held out my right, thumb circling index finger in the classic movie sign for 'papers please'.

He too produced a card from a snazzy gold case;

Sebastian Reid.
Same title.
Same address.

I looked both cards over and again, both sides twice and tried to clear my head. I had a little more knowledge now but it had only given rise to more questions and no small number of imagined crimes and misdeeds and potential law suits. Christa had taken a complete powder. I was marooned.

"What do you guys want," I repeated?

It was the best I could come up with at the time.

"We represent a Mrs. Sandra Elisabeth Williams, of San Francisco," the navy-blue suit said. "We have serious business to discuss with you, Mr. Edgars. Legal business. Can we go somewhere and buy you some lunch perhaps?" He glanced at his watch. "Brunch, I suppose."

While they watched and waited and chewed on the word 'legal' in stereo, my heart sank to the floor. I felt my sphincter clench. Sure, I knew Sandy Williams. I'd fucked Sandy Williams a bunch of times over the course of a crazy week at the beginning of the season. Enjoyed it too and I think she had as well. Been jerking off to the memories since the day she left. Might have been in love with her. Maybe still am. Jealous husband? Maybe. Who knew? I hadn't seen or heard from her in five or six months. Hadn't really expected to ever hear from her again. It had been that kind of thing. I, who made a very good living because of the glib nature of my tongue and my quick wit, had been struck mute.

"Mr. Edgars, the matters we have to discuss are quite..." – he paused to search for just the right word –

"...delicate. They require some privacy. Perhaps a quiet table at the High Times Diner down the road? We'll wait while you change."

He lifted his chin slightly at my sweats. He dripped disdain. What could I do? If they knew me and they knew Sandy Williams and they knew the High Times Diner; if they had serious, even delicate, business to discuss with my sorry self, I knew I was fucked in some unknown but disastrous way. I nodded my assent and went upstairs to change. Fucked again, I thought, but fucked if I knew how.

*

The first time I saw Mrs. Sandra Elisabeth Williams of San Francisco she was sitting in Seat 5, Table 22, in the Abattoir restaurant where I worked as a fine dining waiter. It was very early in the season. We had been through the previews and the gala openings and the red carpets and the parade. The restaurant was ticking smoothly along in low gear, resting for the sprint ahead. The menu had been troubleshot, ironed out, and finalized. Most of the staff returned year after year. The dining room waiters were all friends or at least comrades in arms. We made stupid money. Lunch Wednesdays, dinner Tuesday through Saturday, second seating and after-theatre on Friday and Saturday, Sunday brunch and an early dinner. Thirty hours a week of actual work maybe and, if things worked out, we paid taxes on minimum wage and banked 3 or 4 grand a week in tips. We sweated. We played hard when we were not at work. When Sandy sat in my section everything about the restaurant was shiny new. The squabbles, the love affairs, the exhaustion, the burn out, the breakdowns, they were all still to come. The staff were all fresh as daisies. I was full of piss and vinegar. I had spent most of the winter at a tony wine bar in the city and even managed a month in the islands. I was fighting trim.

Sandy and her friends were my first table of that evening, pre-theatre, in at 5:00 and out by 7:30 to catch the opening curtain of the latest, hottest, must-see musical at 8:00. I remember being pleased to see eight women and no men at the table. I ate tables of women for lunch and the manager knew it. A few compliments, a little flattery, a couple of 'check out my skater's butt' poses, a drink, maybe two each, wine by the glass from the middle of the list, mostly salads and dinner specials, lots of fish and chicken, no dessert because 'I'm watching my weight', separate cheques, good tips, and out the door leaving the table free for the serious dining and serious wine and serious tipping crowd who would arrive for the more leisurely cabaret seating a little after 8:00. Sometimes I threw in a little tantrum-y, *faux* effeminate, gay stuff so they would think I was one of them. Whatever it took. This strategy had worked for me for years.

Sandy caught my eye from the start. She would have caught any man's eye. About my age, early forties, very well preserved. Little yellow patterned sundress with a cornflower blue sweater casually over her shoulders; it was warm enough during the day but cooled down remarkably at night. It was still early in the year. She was classic beautiful like a movie star; Natalie Wood maybe, big brown eyes, shoulder length brown hair, straight with a bit of a flip at the ends, real healthy looking. You just knew it would be baby-soft to the touch. Big fucking diamond like an egg on her married hand. Make up? Not that I could see but she glowed like a pearl. Five foot two maybe, 110 pounds soaking wet, cleavage that belonged on a much larger woman. She seemed shy. She looked at the world in little glimpses from under long lashes. She was in a state of constant semi-blush. On her it was fetching. She looked excited and out of breath and pretty as a picture. I checked my fly, swallowed my breath mint, cleared my throat and approached the table as I had done a million times before and a thousand times since, gave a queer little swoon, grabbed a chair back roughly enough to get their attention, and announced in a voice loud enough for the whole room to hear;

"Well, I guess the boss finally forgives me for banging up his new car, seating a table of eight super-models in my section."

There was much laughter and moaning.

We went from there.

*

Sandy caught my eye from the start. That beautiful face, that full, sincere smile that showed her brilliant white teeth and always that spectacular *décolletage*. I manoeuvred to take the order standing next to her in order to peer down discreetly. Twin white globes, freckled, fat, firm, and lovely. The other women were the ugly step-sisters. Too much make-up, too loud, too silly, too vain. They were invisible to me.

The evening went exactly as I had envisioned. A few compliments, a little flattery, a couple of 'check out my skater's butt' poses, a drink, maybe two each, wine by the glass from the middle of the list, mostly salads and dinner specials, lots of fish and chicken, no dessert because 'I'm watching my weight', separate cheques, good tips, and out the door leaving the table free for the serious dining and serious wine and serious tipping crowd who would arrive for the more leisurely cabaret seating a little after 8:00.

As they rose to leave, I was there. (Rule number one from the boss was to greet the table quickly and always kiss the table goodbye. Make them feel wonderful and warm and valued as they come and as they go and they'll come back again, he said. Who was I to argue? The guy was five years younger than I was, lived in a mansion off Third Street and drove a Hummer.) Sandy was the last to rise, fumbling with her little blue sweater wrap and her purse.

I was there, ever the *gallante*;

"Let me help with that."

I held out my hand for her little purse, tucked it neatly under my arm, took her sweater from her hands and held it for her. She looked up into my eyes from under those lashes for a little bit, long enough to send the initial rush of blood offering to St. Peter, and slowly turned, offering me her back like an expensive gift, like treasure.

I helped aim her arms into the sleeves and ran the sweater slowly up to her shoulders, her exquisite, creamy, nicely muscled shoulders. I gripped her gently, briefly there as if to ensure it wouldn't fall down. Her scent had me panting, insane. The special woman-y way she flipped her hair up out of the way at the collar left me weak at the knees. She turned and fixed me again with those eyes from under those lashes and said in a softish voice;

"A real gentleman. They're hard to find these days."

I smiled my best dimply smile. I had already got the tips I wanted out of her and her friends. I was even being a little sincere.

"All part of the service for a beautiful lady at the Abattoir."

Her friends had disappeared in a cloud of noise and nonsense. The theatre was only a five-minute stroll from the restaurant. I moved to walk with her toward the door, taking the opportunity to put my hand on her again at the small of her back to usher her forward before me. Even in a flowing dress her waist was long and her ass was round. Both were perfect. I should have known. She was so small and delectable. She was your favourite snack. Her scent was making me dizzy.

"You know, we're open for after-theatre dessert and drinks. Maybe you and your friends would like to come back. I could reserve you a nice table in my section if you'd like."

"I don't know about that." She laughed as she spoke. "My friends are pretty early to bed, early to rise. I'll probably just have a night cap at the hotel and turn in."

"Our loss. So where are you staying," I asked?

She paused, a heart beat too long. She was thinking.

"Ouch," I thought.

Too personal. Retreat! Retreat!

"We're staying at the Belmont. Do you know it?"

She saved my life.

"Of course, it's the best in the city," I replied.

That was no lie. Two fifty a night for the basics and full for the entire theatre season.

"I sometimes have my own night cap there," I lied.

I wouldn't have been caught dead at the Belmont.

"Then maybe we'll run into each other again."

"I'd like that, Douglas. That would be fun. Thanks for dinner," she said as if I had cooked it or paid for it or shared it with her instead of just bringing the plates and filling the glasses.

Her scent had me dizzy.

The door swung shut behind her.

"What a fucking babe", I thought to myself as I turned to my duties. "What a splendiferous, fucking babe."

That was as far as I went. I was of an age and a temperament that knew a good and decent woman when I met one and streetwise enough to know that such women were not for me. I worked the night through with her scent in my nostrils and my head in the clouds.

That's how I met Mrs. Sandra Elisabeth Williams, of

San Francisco. Now I was going to have lunch with her lawyers. If I had known it would lead to lawyers, I never would have gone for my fucking night cap at The Belmont. I would have just headed straight down to Bentley's like I always did, a place where everybody knew my name and knew what I drank, a place where I could buy a round and run a tab and nobody liked fucking lawyers.

*

"Shall we walk down to the restaurant", Carruthers, I think, said as I appeared on the front porch? "We can have the car pick us up there after." He lifted his chin at a long, black Town Car parked across the street, tended by a natty little man in the driver's seat.

I was freshly showered and shampooed and teeth brushed and dressed in jeans and rope sandals and an Alice Cooper concert T-shirt. Might as well be comfortable in jail, I had thought to myself, if that was where this was going. I bounced down the front porch stairs ahead of them. I had taken the liberty of a tiny line of eye-opener for each nostril after my shower. I wasn't usually a 'hair of the dog' kind of guy but these were extenuating circumstances. Lately, it seemed, there were extenuating circumstances more mornings than not.

I lived in what used to be a grand old house on Arbour Street, three stories, eight bedrooms, just me and 7 room-mates at $400 a month each, all in, month-to-month, no lease, bring your own cell phone, and don't do anything to attract the cops. I saw Christa in her window at the front of the house on the second floor and gave her a little wave as if to reassure her that everything was normal, everything was just great. It was me going to lunch with these fine lawyer friends of mine. I knew her phone would be red hot in a couple minutes time. I could just hear her. I could hear the replies.

'Doug's gone off with the cops.'

'I knew he should cool it with the coke.'

'Is he selling again?'

'I knew he should ease off the bennies.'

'I just knew it.'

'I told you so.'

*

Unlike the staid and venerable Belmont Hotel where Sandy and her friends were staying, the High Times Diner was a regular haunt of mine, a scummy, long, narrow dive of a restaurant shaped like a box-car a half-block stumble from my front door. It catered to locals instead of the transient theatre-going tourist crowd. Open 24 and 365, it offered the same menu all the time. Any time, night or day, you could get a steak or a grilled cheese or oatmeal or chowder and a stack. It was licensed too. I was feeling like I needed something more of a jump start. The place was nearly empty when we walked in.

"A big Bloody Mary for me, Dish," I said as we walked in. "Not sure about these fellows."

Dish, the waiter/manager/owner (nobody knew exactly where Dish fit in on the High Times org chart) looked up from his newspaper as if from a great distance and gave me the same 'I kill you slow' glare he gave all the regulars he loved and grunted something in reply.

"What would you guys like"?

I turned to include them. I was bustling along now, playing the host. The shower and the coffee and the coke and the anticipation of a stiff drink had already started to work their magic.

"Just coffee. It's still rather early."

One of them spoke for them both.

Sure! I had expected as much. Easy enough for him to say. Easy enough for him to judge. He wasn't getting busted or extradited or arraigned or interrogated or something. He hadn't been out of bed for 45 minutes. He didn't have to be at work in 4 hours. He probably knew what the fuck was going on.

We took the far corner booth by the street and Dish delivered our drinks and dumped the menus and grumbled off muttering about the specials on the board by the door. Here's what I thought I knew about Dish. Dish was an old waiter burnout and a mystery and a local legend. Back way before my time he had been the cock of the walk down at The Abbey until they carted him off one night in a tight little white waiter's jacket. There were rumours, of course. We worked in restaurants. There were always rumours. One rumour had it that he had stabbed a guest in the cheek when the guest had tried to send back his steak. Another claimed that he had whipped out his dick and pissed on a table of guests. Both were unsubstantiated but I thought one of them might be just true enough never to ask Dish outright. He had resurfaced in town after about six months away but since then he just wasn't up to fine dining. Sometimes I wondered if he was up to anything at all. Regardless of his provenance, you had to admire his skills. He never wrote anything down and he never got an order wrong and his tables lacked for nothing. His bartending skills were unsurpassed. Everyone in town had tested him at one time or another. He took it well enough. It was a rite of passage for new customers to try to stump Dish behind the bar and he knew the score. I was sure that he made the best tips in town. I had never been to the High Times when Dish wasn't there, stomping from table to kitchen to bar to table or perched behind the cash register relentlessly reading the newspaper. It was said that he had a room on the second floor above the kitchen but I doubted he ever used it. Some people said he owned the place. Some people said he worked for room and board and tips. Nobody knew anything for sure. Dish was a friend of mine but we weren't very close.

After Dish had taken our order, the three of us made obvious and painful small talk until the food arrived. They asked, first Reid then Carruthers, Carruthers then Reid, open-ended questions about the town, its history, its charm, the theatre, how was business, blah, blah, blah. I tried to keep my end up. I tried for charming, settled for rote and glib. When the food arrived, we made the appropriate noises and assured Dish that everything was superb. He appeared not to care.

I was not quite at the 'something light to eat' part of my morning after recovery process so I grabbed a spear of toast from my plate, poked it into the yolk of an egg, and took a small nibble just so I could say I was eating.

Reid and Carruthers both took a careful bite of something more substantial and in tandem reached for their napkins and wiped their mouths. Fucking dabbers; that's what we called their type at the restaurant. Wiped their mouth after every bite. Worse than average tippers. Lots of special requests. Pains in the ass. They got the bare minimum of service. Probably washed their hands before they pissed.

The arrival of the food and the initial tastings seemed to break the ice. My companions gave each other a pregnant glance and you could almost hear the mental clearing of their respective well-shaven, well tanned, well conditioned throats. It was down to business time. The bell had rung. I gripped my Bloody Mary tighter, raised it toward Dish and nodded. Dish got to the making. Dish had served me breakfast before. Dish knew I usually needed a lot of liquids.

"As we said before, Mr. Edgars, we represent Mrs. Sandra Elisabeth Williams, of San Francisco. Actually, we more properly represent her estate. I do apologize. There is no easy way to break such news. I'll just blurt it out. Mrs. Williams and her husband died on July 13 of this year."

He paused to let that little morsel sink in. I just stared. I felt tomato juice puke rise in my throat. I may have made a squeaky little noise. This was bad and the bad had arrived in an old-fashioned hurry. This was the fucking baddest. I wondered where I had been on July 13. Fucked and fucked, royally and again. That was two months ago. I wasn't sure where I had been two nights ago.

I stared at Reid and then at Carruthers and then at Dish as he arrived to deliver my second Bloody Mary and splash some more coffee around, ignoring my guests' gestures of refusal. That's it, Dish, I thought, do it once while you're at the table. Otherwise you'll just have to come back when the dabbers invariably changed their minds.

I stared and stared and they seemed content to allow this to happen. Reid went back to his Western omelette for a bite and dabbed his lips with his napkin. Carruthers looked out the window. They had all the time in the world. Probably each making a million bucks an hour. From a mile away, I heard the rustle-y shake of Dish's newspaper. The air seemed thick and solid now. I struggled to suck in my breath. I was six years old again and it was the summer of 1967. I saw my Aunt Marie's fat and teary face way down close to mine. I smelt her sour breath. I heard her voice;

"They were killed, Dougy. Your Mom and Dad was killed and they won't be back. You're my little boy now and I'm going to raise you like my own."

From the depths I heard myself ask in a strangled

little boy voice just what I had asked then; "How did they die?"

*

After Mrs. Sandra Elisabeth Williams of San Francisco chased her silly gadabout friends through the swinging door I turned back to my duties. Her table of eight was to be flipped to a twelve for Mr. Garrand, a local and the garrulous owner of a regional chain of flower shops, and some of his friends. Good table, good income, nothing outlandish. I had served him a thousand times. Mr. Garrand always asked for my section and always brought a new joke, usually gross and misogynistic. He thought I enjoyed his jokes. I let him think that. I loved his money and he loved me. We understood each other.

His table ran later than usual that night as I recall. I liked to wine him and dine him and take his money and get him out the door no later than 10:30 to make room for the lucrative 11:00 p.m. after-theatre crowd. The after-theatre seating was easy money, bonus money; some tables just wanted dessert and coffee while the more cosmopolitan would order champagne and a late dinner. Tips went up if you could discuss the play they had just seen with some intelligence. I could. I spent an afternoon in the local library at the beginning of each season, learning the ropes as it were. In all my years in that famous theatre town I had yet to actually see a play nor did I want to but I could discuss them all like nobody's business. I read the condensed notes and all the reviews and I cribbed comments from my tables

<hr>

early in the year and was able to weave all this into a good semblance of culture and discernment and taste.

Mr. Garrand and his friends were getting a little sloppy and had an apparently endless supply of old stories to tell. I kept pouring the house plonk, red and white, emptying the ashtrays and calculating fifteen per cent in my head. About 10:40 Marjorie, the house manager came up as I stood behind the bar surveying my domain and drinking a can of ginger ale and said;

"Looks like Garrand's going to go late tonight. I have an eleven o'clock 10 booked. I was going to give them to Alun."

She backed away, expecting a reaction, perhaps a full-blown fight. Marjorie and I had a history. We worked together but we weren't friends. She hated my laziness, my lackadaisical attitude, and my inattention to the rules. I hated her Puritan work ethic and her butt kissing demeanour toward anyone with a heart-beat. My back went up in Pavlovian response and then back down.

"Sure, Madge," I said. I even squeezed off a bit of a smile. "I could use me some early to bed. I beat the drum long and hard last night. Why don't I just finish off the flower king and beat it."

I followed that with my best down-home, shit-eating grin. She had seen it before and never been fooled. She wasn't now. Her spidey senses tingled. She stared at me for a second, nodded and headed off to check my cash register read. My turning down an after-theatre table and, what's more, allowing Alun, the dilettante and my arch-rival as alpha male of the res-taurant, to scoop it from me was beyond weird. I saw her run my cash read and study it, finally looking over at me and saying;

"Okay, close out flower boy, and you're gone."

I knew she would be thinking this one over for a week and suspicious for a month. Fair enough. I knew I was over four thousand dollars for the night and, now, so did she. No one else in the restaurant would touch me. She probably believed I was as grievously hung over as I implied. She did not approve. We had crossed that bridge many a time, her and I. I made a mental note to make her life a living hell for my next shift or two or three just to keep her on her toes. I casually mentioned to Mr. Garrand that I thought an excellent host such as he would have been taking his guests to The Cafe Down the Street to hear the hot new jazz combo everyone was talking about and before I knew it they were gone, eager as if it had been their idea, and I was an easy $300 and change richer.

I tallied up. It had been a good night. 6 hours worked, 52 covers, a third to the house, six fifty in my pocket and I hadn't even broken a sweat. Time to wash the trail dust down and talk some shit with the working class.

Somewhere between the dining room and the staff change room I came across The Markster, the assistant restaurant manager, with a big pitcher of Cosmos heading for his office to do the books and was per-suaded to sample the latest recipe.

Somewhere between the staff change room and the back door I surprised a couple of bus boys bragging about the wicked dope they were smoking and was persuaded to give it a try or two or three.

Somewhere between the front door and my regular stool and my first pint at Bentley's bar I found myself heading up the street to The Belmont. Even now I don't remember it ever being a conscious decision. Sandy wasn't in my head, not on a level that I was willing or even able to admit. I just turned left instead of right into the night and started putting one foot in front of the other.

*

While The Abattoir Restaurant where I made my living was first class, just behind The Abbey in the local peck-ing order and perpetually ensconced in the national top twenty, The Belmont as a hotel had no peers in our little town. Valet parking, snooty help, fresh flowers everywhere, mints on the pillow, in-house spa and masseuse, you name it. If it was luxurious, The Bel-mont had it and it was probably gold-plated. The Belmont's lobby bar was another story. It was small and dark and dead and dreary and usually had Vivaldi's Suite for the Four Seasons whispering out of corner speakers at every season of the year. The beer was all bottled and expensive – no plebeian draught taps here – the wine list lengthy and priced to the sky. For com-pany you could choose between Chuck, the night bartender, and a few out of town tourist stiffs down from the rooms looking for adventure but too afraid to venture into the dark streets of the safest city in the Western world. I found myself, a little stoned (those busboys had not been lying), a little drunk, a little confused, way in the back corner, sitting in front of the fireplace trying to look as if I belonged and as if I just didn't give a good goddamn.

*

(Here, I must pause and in an explicitly un-authorial way tell you straight up, dear reader, that this was not at all my usual *modus operandi* in affairs of the heart. I was, and had always been, a sexual opportunist, always a scavenger, never a predator. Such carnal sins as I had committed were those of convenience and acquiescence, not of passion. I could barely spell premeditation. I took the female bones the good Lord threw me when he threw them my way but did not go to any great lengths to chase them down. Still, I did all right. I tried to treat women well and never overstay my welcome. I was a gentleman. I opened doors and pulled out chairs. I was funny and a good conversationalist. I always picked up the tab and thought I knew my way around reasonably well between the sheets. I worked hard to satisfy the woman before I took my own pleasure. The fact that I was in this little town for only the seven months of the theatre season then off to parts unknown helped to prevent any long-term entanglements. Fact was, I did not want any entanglements. I made it abundantly clear early that I was not interested in a relationship. I was a ship passing in the night and hoped the woman was too. I enjoyed the occasional company and sexual congress of good-looking and amenable women. I liked fucking and liked being fucked and that was as far as the thought process took me. I lived on a 'one day feast next day famine' diet of curious, young bus girls (although my age was making that more difficult with each passing year), jaded forty-something bartenders and freshly divorced divorcees trying to climb back into the ring. My one experience with what I thought had been true love had not been kind. I shunned love now like a diseased and scurrilous bitch.

Strangely, the nearest I can explain what happened to me that late spring night was that I was already smitten, in some sort of love, with Mrs. Sandra Elisabeth Williams, of San Francisco. The reason I went to The Belmont that night certainly was to find her but it was the first time I had done such a thing. This was different. Sandy was just a table and, once a table left my section, they were gone from my mind, perhaps to appear later in some coke-fuelled masturbatory vision. Every now and again, I might make a point of inviting another waiter into my section to 'check out the sweater meat on that one' but I had not thought to share Sandy. Sandy I kept all to myself. It was Sandy that I wanted to see again when I sat down in front of the fireplace at The Belmont bar. I had given no thought, no lucid thought surely, to what would happen if, and when, she appeared.

Nor could I blame my actions on the liquor or the pot. I was not impaired. My tolerance, built up over years of constant, long, and hard practise, was very high. I had done nothing out of the ordinary that day. I woke late and hung over because that is how I invariably woke on any Saturday morning that followed a Friday night. I had a BLT on toasted brown and a vodka and orange for breakfast then another vodka and orange for dessert. I had smoked a tiny bowl of hash on the deck with a room-mate and enjoyed some sun before I had to go to work. Another vodka and orange to get me through the shower and the ironing of a fresh work shirt. I did two short lines of coke the better to enjoy the short walk to work.

I had stopped to eat a souvlaki and catch up on the local scuttlebutt with Gus, the proprietor of my favourite street meat wagon. I knew it was important to eat. I ate when I could, piling it in during the day and going without at work and afterward. At work, I had chugged my usual 4 ounces of vodka from a bottle in my locker just before service in order to loosen my tongue and did a couple of more short lines in the staff john between the dinner and cabaret seatings just to keep my edge. Sometimes, if I had had a particularly long, late night before, I fortified myself with a handful of bennies but, when I did that, I had learned to cut back on the booze because the combination of the two made me sloppy and uncoordinated and slurred my speech. A couple of drinks with The Markster and some weed with the bus boys and I was just feeling right, just another day at the office. I didn't usually get down to any serious drinking until after work but then all bets were off.)

*

Out of the resultant mellow haze in which I sat, halfway pondering my blankness and my confusion,
halfway wondering what the actual fuck I was doing
and how long I would continue to do it, she appeared.
Blue sweater on and buttoned now as it had turned
chilly outside, looking more beautiful than I remembered. A young-ish Natalie Wood, for sure, but with a
better body. Her cheeks were in rose bloom from the
stroll home from the theatre. The ugly step-sisters had
been abandoned.

"Are you enjoying your night cap?"

Her voice was a song, huskier than you would ex-
pect from such a little frame. A little Stevie Nicks, a
little Nico with The Velvet Underground.

"Yes, but I'd enjoy it more if you had one with me."

I was stuck in some lame Rock Hudson and Doris
Day conversation mode. My grin felt like it would split
my face but I couldn't stop. I had lost control of important things.

"That sounds lovely. I'll have what you're having."

Her voice was a song, smoky, like that chick from
The Cowboy Junkies.

I was sipping my favourite, night-time, sitting in an
expensive bar, trying to make time with a woman,
sipping drink. Stinger. Triple. Half brandy, half peppermint crème de menthe. Lots of booze, shaken with
ice, strained, served in a short glass; deadly strong
and great for your breath. I turned to whistle up Chuck
and asked for two more of the same, giving him a little

snot while I was at it. Best waiter at the second-best restaurant in town trumped the night bartender in the dingy bar of the best hotel in town any day and he knew it. Bartenders in our town were just waiters who couldn't handle the pace of working the tables. They were the has-beens and the never-weres. They were halfway out to pasture. The next step down was an assistant manager gig and from there they were gone to work retail or sell real estate. They were held in contempt. They knew it. They understood.

As we were served she had tossed her sweater onto the arm of the leather sofa and released those amazing breasts – much to my delight her nipples had appeared; pert, lovely, chill night blooming. She settled next to me on the couch in front of the fire filling the air all round us with that inexplicable scent of hers and gripping her snifter in both hands, knees prim together like a school girl. I asked her name. We exchanged Sandy and Douglas and then, instead of continuing with the usual bullshit, the 'how did you enjoy the play', sizing things up banter, from out of nowhere I blurted out how beautiful I thought she was and how her husband was a very lucky man and how I envied him. Stoned. Definitely horny. Just trying to be charming. Infatuated. Overcome. Out of my fucking mind. I had lost control of important things.

Even now, even after everything that has happened since, I can honestly say that I meant nothing by it. The booze and the pot and the adrenaline of work and testosterone and the mystery and the scent of her had flipped me into some unlikely, unaccustomed, unfamiliar honesty mode and I was just calling them like I saw them. I figure that I figured in my alcoholic, drug-addled innocence or stupidity that a beautiful woman would want to hear it acknowledged just as I liked to have people compliment me on a styling haircut or a new earring or tattoo or pair of shoes or even a job well done. I could, even this far into the game, have walked away from the situation with a kiss on the cheek and considered it a night well spent. Sandy was a bright, twinkling star a million miles above me. I was the cave man contemplating the heavens for the first time. I was content just to sit there in front of the fireplace and enjoy the smell of her. I was content just as I would be to simply to stare at a beautiful painting, not dreaming of owning it. Content to read the same beautiful passage of a novel over and again. Content to play the same song on repeat because it would have moved me to tears had I been capable of such a feat.

"Thank you," she said.

She took a decent pull at her Stinger. Her tongue slipped out to caress an errant drop from her top lip. Oh my! Such a tongue.

"I do feel beautiful here tonight, with a handsome man in front of a nice fire drinking this wonderful drink after a wonderful dinner and a wonderful play and now that my friends are finally gone to bed."

She smiled me a 'you know how tiring some friends can be even if you love them dearly' little smile. I smiled it right back at her although I had no friends to speak of and so never tired of them at all. I said nothing. Handsome! Had she just called me handsome? The fire was catching the highlights and shadows of her hair just so. I was enchanted.

"I wonder though, if he does, if my husband thinks he's lucky...in that sense of the word."

She took another pull at her drink and licked her lips just so. The bottom lip this time then the top. We stopped then to contemplate the fire and consider just what she might have meant by this enigmatic comment. Kate Jackson, I thought! She has a Kate Jackson mouth. I hearkened back to my teenage bedroom and my Charlie's Angels poster on the wall and how, when my peers were freaking for Farrah Fawcett, I was a rabid and vocal Kate Jackson man and proud of it. That full, sensuous bottom lip and the merest hint of a thin top. Did it for me then, does now, always will. I found a voice. I found words. I was Cary Grant again. I had lost control of some important things.

"Your husband doesn't know what he has then. He must be a fool. If you were my wife....".

Where the hell had that come from? The idea of me with a wife had occurred to me just once before, died a bitter death, and been buried deep. I let the thought trail off. I was adrift. I was without a destination. I was over my head about a million miles, the Marianas Trench below me and I could barely swim. She looked carefully around the fire pit and then fixed on me most intently.

"And if you were my husband, Douglas," she said,

"what would you do now, here, under these circumstances?"

She gestured slightly with her chin, taking in all that was around us, the canned Vivaldi, the room, the world, the fire, the night. In for a penny, in for a pound, I heard my aunt say, one of a million tortured aphorisms and folksy sayings she would spout on any occasion. They were my entire legacy from her. I found words. I found a voice.

"I would sit here a while and enjoy the fire and this drink and maybe another drink besides. I would enjoy the way you look and the way you sound and the way you smell tonight. Then I would take you upstairs to our room and make love to you as best as I was able and then stroke your hair and whisper to you until you fell asleep."

She looked at me then again for the longest time. Too deep. Too long. I felt drops of blood form on my forehead. I scrambled back to my Catholic college days and remembered my little shock of Bible study lore – *Mene mene tekel upharsin*. I wondered how Cary Grant would have extracted himself from this delicate mess. Sandy took another tiny sip from her snifter, repeated the trick with her tongue and her lips, first bottom then top, fixed my soul again with her eyes, smiled a mostly sad little smile and said;

"I've always wondered what that would be like."

So, I was lost.

*

"You have our condolences, Mr. Edgars.

The lawyers again.

"Mrs. Williams and her husband, Gary were killed as a result of an act of random violence," Reid or Carruthers continued.

The world was becoming fuzzy for me. My hearing was not what it had once been. My sight was down by about half. The glass at the end of my arm was an iceberg. I thought I might be sweating. Shivering too maybe. I had no way of knowing for sure.

"They were driving to the opening of an art show in San Francisco. They were stopped at a red light. A young man fleeing the police after a robbery car-jacked them. Mr. Williams was pulled from the driver's seat and shot twice in the head. He died at the scene. Mrs. Williams became a hostage. She died some time later in a shootout of sorts. She was shot by a police sniper. Accidentally."

He paused to look at his silent colleague as if he could vouchsafe the story and then at me. I was intent on my Bloody Mary and breathing and some things out the window.

"We have the documentary evidence if you'd care to look it over, Mr. Edgars."

"No!"

Too loud. My volume control had gone south. My brain was liquid. I had half-expected them to offer me autopsy photos. They were that kind of lawyers. They were that kind of men. You just knew.

"Where we, our firm, comes into the picture, Mr. Edgars, is as the executors of the Williams' estate.

Normally, in situations such as this, and by that, I mean the premature death of prominent, respected, and wealthy citizens like the Williams, the last will and testament is a complicated document, often running to several volumes, with appendices in some cases. The Williams' documents, some of them at any rate, were another matter altogether."

His tone told me in spades that I was not considered part of the prominent, respected, and wealthy class. His tone told me that I might never understand such a thing as this. He paused to let me catch up. He chanced another look to his back-up. Dish was back at my elbow with another drink and another refill for the fun twins. Had I ordered that?

"Everything all right, Douglas?"

My head jerked up. I had not been aware that Dish had ever known my name. He had never let on that he did. I would never have guessed, not from the disdain he showed every time I walked in and the disgust he showed as I left after having left some astronomical tip. Wake the kids. Phone the neighbours. This was a day for the ages.

"Yah, we're fine, Dish. Just got some bad family news, legal news."

I grimaced as if that explained the whole odd tableau.

"Lawyers, huh? They're incubators for bad news. Like doctors. You don't have to tell me twice."

Dish was being positively loquacious now. He gave my new friends his steak knife glare and was gone.

Still amazed that Dish had deigned to give me an extra word not related to my food or drink or my bill, I turned back to Reid and Carruthers. Dish had given me strength. I sucked in a huge draft of air.

"So, what exactly are you guys telling me here? Sandy's dead, I got that, and that hurts like hell. She was good, good people. She was world class. Her husband probably was too. But why do I all of a sudden need lunch with two lawyers?"

"We began the probate of the will on July 17."

That was Reid. He looked to Carruthers to confirm this pertinent fact. Carruthers nodded. Carruthers had turned into the strong, silent type. Carruthers was pissing me off. I entertained a short, vivid fantasy of smashing my drink glass into his cheekbone.

"We do not know the details of your relationship with Mrs. Williams, Mr. Edgars, nor do we care to know. The nature of that relationship simply is not germane to the task at hand. We have merely been following the dictates of her will. Therefore, as instructed by that document, we have been working for the past four weeks to fulfill the stipulations therein."

Puking would seem a tremendous relief right now, I thought. I would like to puke until I was empty in both heart and gut and soul. I placed the long-forgotten piece of toast on the edge of my plate, gently like it was glass or dangerous. I wouldn't be needing it any more. I wondered if I'd ever need solid food again.

I had become a task at hand.

I was having a meal with men who used words like

'therein' and 'fleeing' in the course of ordinary conversation.

A woman who had smelled like flowers and of whom
I had never tired had been killed and Dish knew my
name and had acted sympathetic.

I was through the looking glass.

"You have passed the several tests she instructed
us to conduct. Mr. Edgars. You, therefore, become Mrs.
William's sole heir and, because she was pre-deceased
by her husband, his sole heir as well. He, you see, left
everything to her. She left it all to you."

He dabbed his lips and pushed back in his seat as if
he had just explained everything from the origin of the
species to the exact date of the second coming of
Christ. He looked inordinately proud of his erudition.
He looked to his companion in triumph as if he expected a high-five or a come-to-Jesus Hallelujah. I
stared blankly all around me at nothing at all and
wished for a little piece of another world, any other
world than what I had going on right now. Death by
drowning sounded attractive.

*

Sandy and I passed another half-hour give or take
talking about this and that, the play she saw that evening and the ones she had already seen and the
restaurants in which she had dined. The tone of the
rest of the night appeared to have been settled. To be
honest, I suppose, Sandy talked and I merely filled in
some of the blanks. I barely kept my end up. My mind

was a million miles away and going a million miles an hour. I had not thought so much, so deeply, so long, in years. I was consumed with being smitten, staring like some yokel at a skyscraper. She was that to me. She definitely resembled a young Natalie Wood, I thought, but with better skin. I searched her face for the slightest imperfection and found none. Just some crinkling activity around the eyes when she smiled that made her beauty almost painful to behold. Vivaldi churned on in the background. Finally, my brain gave it up and at what I hoped was a convenient juncture I pressed the issue. Gun to my head, I pulled the trigger. The pot or the third Stinger or the testosterone got the best of me.

"Would you like to go upstairs now?"

Again, that look, too deep, too long by half. I was certain in that instant that she was going to call my bluff.

("Douglas Edgars, the joke's on you," with huge guffaws from the studio audience and the buxom starlet being ushered off the stage and me left to explain to Bill Cosby or Wink Martindale that I had known what the game was all along and was not really a complete fool.)

It was not that way at all. She drained her Stinger, primly wiped her fingers on the embossed napkin, dropped it in a careful heap beside her glass, heaved a great sigh which pushed out her breasts alarmingly and, standing, said quietly;

"In for a penny, in for a pound."

She fixed me with a gentle smile, a kind smile, and reached down for my hand.

So, I was lost.

*

Now that we were down to business, Carruthers seemed to take on new life. The other one had sketched the broad strokes and remained only to provide moral support or strong-arm back-up in case the crazed waiter flipped at the news. Carruthers placed a briefcase on the bench seat between them, propped it open and started shuffling papers. I could smell expensive leather and the stale breathy air of airplanes. He seemed content now that we had gotten to the paperwork and had left silly human emotion in the dust. He was in his element. Even in the cracked faux leather booth by the window of the High Times Diner, even across the world from his San Francisco office, his briefcase made it so.

"By the terms of the will, as was mentioned, Mr. Edgars, you are the sole heir of a rather substantial estate."

He gave Reid a curt nod as if to acknowledge his Herculean efforts in bringing the matter this far.

"Mrs. Williams' instructions were very precise, and somewhat peculiar, if I might add."

He was in familiar territory now. His voice was a legal instrument. I was staring at him like he was an animal in the zoo, suddenly become sentient and conversational. He looked up from the safety of the briefcase and gave me a little smile that I might find him human and approachable. I did not. The ambient traffic noise, the vibrations of the window and the colours of my Bloody Mary held my attention fast. He motored on, oblivious. This was the can-do sticktoitiveness by which he set his watch every morning. He was in his natural element, a fish in deep, calm water. His briefcase had given him life. His briefcase held all the answers. All hail the briefcase. I blinked a couple of times and hoped that I wasn't becoming mad.

"Now, please understand that I am presenting this information in the order outlined in Mrs. Williams' will. She was really quite specific. She left us no choice in the matter."

He was letting me know that things would have been much different, and better, had he and his briefcase been in charge. You could tell that he liked to be in charge. He liked the trains to run on time. I blinked a couple of times and hoped that I wasn't becoming mad.

More smile from him.

More window for me.

More Bloody Mary?

Where the hell was Dish?

"Mrs. Williams asked first that we verify certain facts before these final bequests were made. She provided us with some instances, some examples if you will, from your life, instances which I presume she had from you at some point, and she asked us to determine their veracity. This our investigative staff have done over the course of the last four weeks. They were very thorough and I am pleased to say that your story passed in all particulars. If it hadn't, the estate would have been distributed instead across several local charities. Your story checked out, as they would say in the gangster movies."

He gave me that, 'I must be human after all, I just made a joke' look and attempted something with his mouth that approximated a grin. I stared at him as if he were an alien approaching with a large anal probe. Verify their veracity? What the fuck? He rambled on. He had hit the wall. He had burst right through. His briefcase made it so.

"Orphaned at seven, raised by a spinster aunt until her death in 1984, university degree, magna cum laude, some graduate school, no criminal record, no previous marriages nor offspring, a good, albeit lengthy, employment history, no financial record to speak of, for good nor ill."

My life in a nutshell.

I swallowed so that I would not puke on the table.

"Having determined that you are what and who you apparently told her you were, we can now move on to the fulfillment of the other aspects of Mrs. Williams' final document. Again, I remind you that my colleague and I are following the stipulations of Mrs. William's last will and testament exactly. It was, is, a peculiar document. I have handled hundreds such situations in my time. I thought I was immune to surprise. I was mistaken."

He shrugged.

I stared.

He handed me over a fat yellow-brown envelope, the expensive, fancy kind that closed with a bit of elastic looped around a cardboard wheel.

"This envelope contains one hundred thousand dollars in an assortment of used bills, nothing larger than a hundred. Mrs. Williams was quite specific about the amount and the denominations and the format. Please don't ask how we managed to get this much cash over the several boundaries that we did. It upsets our digestion. My friend here was quite beside himself on the flight here."

That almost human smile again.

That grin.

I felt murder in my heart. I felt the long muscles in my thighs clench as they made ready to leap.

The talking one glanced briefly at the other one – they were wholly interchangeable to me now or perhaps they kept switching seats when my head was turned – who smiled the smallest possible smile in return and then back at me again. Fight or flight or freeze. Who knew? I was out the window. I was long distance. The quiet one was unaccustomed to such informality, such familiarity. He began stirring his coffee as if his life depended on it. Perhaps it did. Who knew what happened once you were through the looking glass? Alice had never been very specific. I blinked a couple of times and hoped that I wasn't becoming mad.

"This envelope contains the deed to a property here in town."

He stopped to consult a legal pad.

"160 King's Landing. You own that now. I will need your signature a few times, of course, in order to make that official."

A second envelope was placed carefully, reverently, in front of me with the first, one atop the other. I heard the kiss and the jingle of keys. It hurt the insides of my ears like a scream. He pressed on.

"There are two vehicles in the garage. They were both purchased and placed there by terms of the will. They're yours too."

Another yellow-brown envelope.

Carefully.

Reverently, so as not to slide.

Just so.

Another painful jingle of keys.

"This envelope contains an American Express card in your name. This particular brand of card is euphemistically referred to as an 'American Express Black'. Officially, such 'black' cards do not exist. If, as they say, you have to ask, you can't afford it. There is no credit limit attached to this card, not in the usual sense. You could buy a small country or two with it if you liked and the bill would be paid promptly and in full at the end of each month by the accounting staff of my firm. It actually says that in the document itself, 'a small country or two'."

Bemused, he paused and looked to me for an explanation. One was not forthcoming. I was not feeling in a very giving mood. Where have I heard those words before, I thought to the window? He gave me another small, questioning smile. I was giving nothing back. My mind was full of the way Sandy's vertebrae made a soft, pink ladder down her back, from the nape of her neck to the flare and the swell of her buttocks. My mind was full of the smell of her, the smell of sex and flowers and magic, that smell I smelled when I woke beside her in bed, that smell I smelled sometimes for an instant before I realized I had woken up alone.

"When all is taken into account, Mr. Edgars, with stocks and bonds and the very extensive real estate portfolio and the art....Oh my goodness, the art. We haven't even touched on the art. Would you like to see the art?"

He looked to his companion.

"Do we have time?"

He reached into the briefcase again. Did he have autopsy pictures in that briefcase? His colleague, his helpmate, gave him a look of surprised disapproval. The forgetting of things was obviously just not done. It violated some lawyerly code. When all was taken into account, I wanted to kill them both but I could not lift my eyes from the envelope pile, much less my arms. I was an infant. I was a paraplegic. I was a blob of some strange goo. I looked at the remnants of a Bloody Mary in a glass at the end of some fleshy stem near me. Who in the hell had finished my Bloody Mary? As if to solve the crime, Dish was there in a second. I spoke. My voice was distant, an octave higher than usual like I was excited.

"Another Bloody Mary please Dish. Better double it up."

Dish left. I heard my voice again to Reid/Carruthers, an octave lower than usual as if I was just getting over a cold.

"How did you say she died?"

Sandy shot in a police shootout? Accidently? By a sniper? What the actual fuck? That wasn't right. That couldn't possibly be right. That would never in a million, million years ever be right. I wanted to tear the world to pieces with my fingers. I wanted to bite the world with my teeth.

*

I tossed a fifty onto the fireplace table for Chuck. Chuck was engrossed in the CNN bottom-of-the-screen headline roll on the silent TV above the bar and led Sandy to the back stairs. Chuck never looked at us. We didn't look at Chuck.

The Belmont building was one block square and squat and three stories tall. A local ordinance forbade building any building higher than that in our picturesque little theatre town. Ruined the view or some such thing. I had never given it any thought. I had never given a shit. The elevators were at the front left from the street entrance, main desk and offices to the right and, away in the back, past the dingy bar, were some all but forgotten stairs that went up to the rooms. I had worked as part of a catering crew here a couple of times. I knew my way around pretty well.

We mounted the stairs and just as we rounded the

landing toward the second flight, just as we were lost to sight from the deserted lobby, I reached for Sandy's hand, spun her gently around, and pulled her to me. She was poised on the first step up and I was a step below so we came together nose to nose. I felt a need to kiss this woman immediately. It was a hunger. Kiss we did. If it had been the movies, the violins would have started just then, followed by the cellos and the French horns and the relentless bassoons. I felt quite insane.

Her lips were soft and firm and full and perfect against mine. I felt the sweet pressure of her breasts against my chest. I had caught her unawares, about to speak I think, or perhaps about to draw a breath, because her mouth was open somewhat when I planted mine. A brief press then a brief pull back to reseat. I put my hand to her cheek and leaned in harder. In time I felt the whisper of her tongue on mine, soft and wet and warm and tasting of Stinger. We held that kiss for a count of two or ten or two thousand. I released her, pushing her away, sucking gently on her bottom lip as I withdrew. I had never been kissed up to that point in my life. Never will be again.

"My friends, Douglas...."

Her voice was soft, insistent, calm. I was a recalcitrant child. She was the patient teacher. She took my hand in hers and turned to pull me up the steps. I held my ground. With her some three and a half or four steps above me, her hand extended but still linked in mine, I pulled to slow and stop her. I stood firm.

"Sandy. Wait."

"We'll be more comfortable in my room. And more private."

She pulled again, laughing.

"No, wait."

I would not be deterred. I stood firm. I walked up a step or two past her and pulled her up to the next landing. I took her in my arms and kissed her again. Hard and fierce this time. I pushed her up against the wall. One hand down the smooth, soft back of her to the swell of her rump. The other hand around the front to cup a perfect pillow of a breast and give it a gentle squeeze. I kissed her, hard and fierce this time. She responded in kind, one hand in my hair to hold me close, the other on my shoulder for balance. We were both breathing hard now, breathing in hitches, sucking for air. We were uncoordinated, unsteady, the both of us making rude little noises, smacks of lip and slaps of saliva. She sucked my tongue hard into her mouth. I felt a jolt like lightning. I may have moaned. Perhaps she did. We broke. I put my hands one on each shoulder pinning her to the wall and looked down at her. Her lips were wet. Red. Swollen.

I made to speak. Did I have some romantic overture for this delicate juncture? Something from Noel Coward or Shakespeare or even something from Bogie to Bacall?

No!

Best I could come up with was;"I've been thinking of doing that since I first saw you."

"I believe you," she laughed. "I guess that's why you messed up my dinner order."

She leaned in to kiss me again. This time it was her mouth doing the kissing, her hands on my chest holding us upright against the wall. It was her up on her toes. I had become the victim, the prey.

"Come on, Mister. I don't want to be on the front page of the local paper tomorrow morning canoodling with my new boyfriend."

She turned and trotted up the stairs, yellow sundress hem bouncing behind her.

She giggled.

I was paralyzed.

Screwed up her dinner order? No way! My waiter vanity flared.

New boyfriend! Had she called me her boyfriend?

My cock was so hard a cat couldn't have scratched it.

I was a child at Christmas. I was excited, anxious, poised at the top of the roller coaster drop. I was giddy. I was breathless. I chased her up the stairs best as I could in my condition.

*

Reid/Carruthers took me through it all again. You had to admire their patience. I suppose they were accustomed to dealing with suddenly catatonic, suddenly rich young heirs gone brain dead, slurping Bloody Marys as if their lives depended on it, and asking questions for which there were no ready answers. There was probably a whole course about it in law school. These guys had obviously aced it. These guys probably taught the course *pro bono* down at their local city college.

I was lucky. They did not have autopsy pictures after all but rather newspaper clippings detailing the sensational and macabre events of July 13. These I read carefully, faltering only at the photo of the victims, a posed studio shot of Sandy and an older gentleman, the late Walter I assumed, about whom I knew so many intimate secrets and who presumably had never heard of me at all. I was killing time. I leafed through the clippings again, slower this time. I skimmed here, read a bit there. I wandered a bit in the corridors of my mind. I may have slept off and on or lost consciousness for brief moments. I quietly went insane, just me and the newspaper clippings and my memories. At some point during this process, one of the lawyers had moved to the bench beside me and was holding me around the shoulders as I sobbed for the first time in my life. I hadn't wept for my parents that I could recall. I hadn't wept for my Aunt Marie. I hadn't wept over my own broken heart. Dish was nowhere to be seen. We were alone it seemed, we three. We were all alone on the planet. We were all alone. Some of us were crying into the newspapers. Some were looking uncomfortable and doing unaccustomed things. I suspected I had been cut off. I wondered if the lawyers were going to pick up the bill. I wondered if they would leave a sufficient tip for Dish.

When my crying jag was over, Reid or Carruthers led me through the will again. I had passed their stupid tests and now all of Sandy's money was mine. She had bought me a house I had told her I loved and filled the garage with dream cars to my specifications. She had given me an envelope stuffed with greenbacks and a mythical American Express card with my name on it because I had laughed at the one with hers. I owned all of her houses and furniture and automobiles and stocks and bonds and her paintings and art pieces. I had laughed too when she called them pieces and mocked her in what I imagined to be an upper crust accent and she had pretended to be angry until I was buried in her again for the millionth time and neither of us could be angry anymore. She had written me a letter – Jesus! How I had missed the mention of the letter the first time around? – explaining all of this and the letter and everything else was all neatly packed into a black leather briefcase that was mine to keep as a lovely parting gift. All of this was mine and I would have traded it all in an instant for another single sniff of the baby fine hairs at the nape of her neck.

The lawyers talked as lawyers are trained and paid to talk. I was lost. I wandered. I felt hot and I shivered and I was quite insane. I babbled, I think. I know that I made noises and I remember laughing, too long, too loud, at something. The lawyers did not laugh. Dish was nowhere to be found. We were alone, Reid and Carruthers and I. We were a cozy little party of three and one of us was quite insane. Somewhere in the midst of all the frivolity and the tears a lawyer jerked his chin at another lawyer and said in quite a different voice than he had been using with me; "Make the call, Bill".

Lawyer Bill had wandered off toward the bathrooms murmuring into a cell phone the size of his business card. A lawyer stayed with me. He spoke to me. His voice was quiet. I liked the sound of it. It was quiet.

"You're obviously going to need some time, Mr. Edgars, to absorb all of this. I've taken the liberty of having my colleague call The Abattoir and explain that you've had some bad tidings and won't be in to work tonight. He'll do it in a manner that does not reveal the particulars. We have every reason to be discreet. I know tomorrow is usually a day off for you. You have a lot to think about. You have plans to make. Like it or not, your life has been changed. I'm sorry that we had to spring all of this on you the way we did. I wish there could have been some easier, softer way. We will stay with you until things are a little more settled, until you've had time to process the changes. You will eventually have to come to San Francisco to sign some papers, rather a lot of papers to be sure. It would be best if you were to give some serious thought to taking a week or two off to wrap your head around all of this."

I could barely nod. Hearing him using this jargon was like watching Mr. Rodgers shoot smack. I grimaced instead. How did he know tomorrow was my day off? I didn't want to go to San Francisco. I didn't want to sign rather a lot of papers to be sure. I wanted to curl up on the bench seat and rest. Everything about me was tired.

"Like it or not, your life has been changed. Irrevocably changed. All of this change will have to be explained to your friends and co-workers here. We can help you with a cover story if you like or you can tell everyone the whole truth."

He uttered this last like it would be an unfortunate last resort.

"We're going to be in town for a while yet, until you say it's okay to go. We work for you now. You will have to come to San Francisco at some point, the sooner the better actually. You have a mountain of paper to sign there and decisions to be made."

He was beginning to repeat himself in his rush to comfort me. I was not at all comforted. I weighed 10,000 pounds. I was finding it difficult to breathe. Blinking was a painful labour. I had forgotten how to swallow.

"Now, how about we take you back to your apartment, make sure you're comfortable and arrange to meet again in the morning to flesh out some of the details? We're staying at The Belmont. We heard it's the best in town. Do you know it?"

I bolted. I was in the parking lot and the puking that had been threatening for so long had come to be. Long, looping heaves of bile and coffee and vodka and tomato juice and little toast bits that left me breathless and crampy and sore. Reid/Carruthers was there too, to hand me an embossed handkerchief to wipe my pukey lips and snotting nose.

"I think I want to be alone now," I said when I had caught my breath.

I came up off my knees and tried to look steady.

They exchanged a glance and one of them handed me the briefcase stuffed with my new life and said he understood. It was clear that he did not. We arranged to meet for breakfast the next day at 9:00 in The Belmont dining room. I stumbled off through the parking lot, my new black leather accessory dangling from my hand, slapping my rubbery thigh at every step. The sun was preternaturally bright. The cars were deafening loud as they rushed past. The sidewalk was chalky and sticky and soft. I could see my house just up the street a million miles away.

I'm drunk, I thought. I'm drunker than I've ever been before. I'm high as a kite on some beautiful, awful new drug to which I have become addicted and it will kill me and I will be happy when death arrives. I will kiss Death and usher Death in. I will sit Death down in a comfy chair. I will bring Death some slippers. I will put the kettle on. I'm drunk I thought. I've had some bad tidings. I finally knew how it felt to have bad tidings. Having bad tidings felt exactly like God had kicked you right square in the junk.

*

Sandy was in Suite 304, left, down the hall, at the end, in the corner. A sitting area with a couple of tiny couches and a TV and mini fridge bar thing and closed doors to the bedroom and the bath. I knew there would be a tiny balcony just behind those heavy curtains.

Finally inside, did we tear at each other's clothes and make it in a frenzy with her draped clumsily over the arm of the sofa? Not hardly. Everything was different with Sandy. Everything was better with Sandy. Sandy was her own time zone. Sandy was her own planet. She pulled me gently in and closed and locked and chained the door.

"Please sit down," she said. "Make yourself comfortable."

Like an automaton, I pulled off my blazer – a steal at $9.00 at the Salvation Army thrift store downtown – and flopped onto the nearest nearby faux leather with a squeak and a puff of old hotel air. I was quite breathless. I was sweating. I could feel my pulse in my cock. She tossed her sweater after my coat and sat close beside me, knees together, turned slightly toward me, pretty as a picture. Taking both my clammy monster hands in her small cool ones she gathered them in her lap and pressed them together there firm.

"I want to talk to you before we do anything, Douglas. What's going to happen is going to happen. I've already decided that and I'm very stubborn when my mind is made up."

She smiled at me then and I saw what she had looked like as a little girl. I knew she had always been the prettiest girl in class. I knew that the other girls tried to hate her for it but couldn't. She had shone and she had smiled and she had beat the other girls down with her shine and her smile. I knew the whole neighbourhood had loved her. I knew she had been the apple of her father's eye.

"Well, my mind is made up about you and about me and about this. There's no going back."

She raised her chin an inch at the room as if offering it to me for sale. The ceiling light had made the room very bright. She was radiant. I felt wretched and poor and less than anything.

"Before it happens though, I want you to understand why. I don't want you to think I'm some kind of....tart. The truth is, you're going to be only my second man, my second lover, and I want us to know each other before that happens."

With this last she leaned in, placed one palm on each of my cheeks, and gave me another kiss to curl my toes and leave me blind.

"...but now I'm going to say something I've never said before and will quite likely never say again, something I've only heard before in the movies and not very good movies at that."

She paused for dramatic effect.

"Excuse me please while I slip into something more comfortable. Will you mix us a drink of something? All this kissing and stuff has left me positively parched or maybe I'm just turning into a lush. Or maybe I'm just scared."

She smiled again to break my heart and then she was gone through the bedroom door. I stepped to the bar and got busy with the familiar tools of my trade. Behind me I heard the sound of water soft running and, after a while, the clatter of heavy wood hangers.

*

By the time I got home from the diner and the lawyers, the house was deserted and dark. The eight of us housemates all worked in the restaurant business in some capacity. Sunday was a busy night with diners coming in early straight from the matinee performances for a last quick holiday bite before their getaway trip home. It was an easy night too, no cabaret seating in most places and no after theatre. By nine the restaurants would all be locked up tight and dark and the downtown bars would be full of thirsty pent-up waiters and busboys and cooks. There was no theatre at all on Mondays so all of the high-end restaurants were closed. No one worked on Monday. Sunday night was our Saturday night, our entire weekend compressed. Sunday night was the time to pull out all the stops, time to drink and drug away a whole week's worth of stress and disappointment and joy and despair. Sunday night was the time to approach that new woman or seek out that once-discarded old for *auld lang syne*. On Sunday night anything was possible. Come closing time, the late-night booze cans would be hopping. For the town dealers it was Black Friday in a boom town.

I made straight for my room and locked the door behind me. The house was a vacuum. I needed noises. Tossing the briefcase onto the bed, I moved to the stereo and searched for a disc, finally settling on the new Warren Zevon release. Just came out, nothing there to remind me of anything, certainly nothing there to remind me of the late, great Sandy. I smiled at the thought. She would have found that funny, she loved puns and silly wordplay. She had been much better at it than me. The first notes took me to the memory of dancing with her in that hotel room that first night or maybe the next hotel room the night after that. The first notes took me to the feel of her in my arms, just swaying slowly together, smelling her, drawing in her lithe, lean form. God! I had loved that she was so small.

I did a fat, long line, the kind of line I'd cut for my best friend on his birthday.

Stripping off my sweaty, puke smelling clothes, I tossed them toward the hamper and sat on the bed in my boxers. I didn't have a lot of choice when it came to places to sit. My room contained only an ancient thrift store futon mattress on the floor and a rickety folding card table for my stereo and my laptop, a chair, a laundry hamper, and two battered suitcases out of which I mostly lived. My low seniority in the house meant that my room did not come with a closet nor a window. I shared a bathroom down the hall with Christa, the luscious-nippled lesbian and Glen, a furiously gay *garde-manger* at the Abattoir. I opened the black briefcase carefully on my lap and went through the contents for the third time, carefully avoiding the picture of the happy couple, one half of whom I had introduced to the intricacies and pleasures of oral sex, much to our prolonged and mutual delight. I skipped her letter too in its crisp little envelope with a fancy, cursive 'D' scrawled on it in some expensive, obsidian ink. The picture would surely drive me mad. The letter was sure to kill me. The letter was a ticking bomb.

I did a fat, long line, the kind of line I'd cut if I'd just won the lottery.

I opened the first envelope and spilled its contents onto the bed beside me. Neat, banded bundles of ratty old bills. I had told Sandy once that if I ever got my hands on that much cash I would toss it on the bed and fuck it. Fucking the money didn't seem like much of a plan now. I swept it back into the briefcase and withdrew the envelope containing the car keys. I squeezed them through the paper. I felt their sharp edges with the ball of my thumb.

I did a fat, long line, the kind of line I'd cut for a first-time girlfriend.

I reached for a bottle of plum brandy. I had acquired a taste for it from a Yugoslavian friend of mine a long time back and since then had kept a bottle by my bed for late night go-to-sleeps and the occasional early morning wake-me-up. It was thick and sweet and powerful like drinking lava. Sandy had asked one evening what kind of car I would drive if I could choose any one.

"I think a real man needs two sets of wheels, actually," I had replied, half in jest. I had never even considered owning a car. I didn't drive.

We were naked, face to face, the hard length of me squeezed between us. The air was full of the aroma of our sex and I was high and stupid from it. I was playing the fool.

"A real man," I went on, "needs a truck, a big-assed four-wheel drive Dodge Ram sort of pick-up truck with a lift kit and great big tires and chrome everything for when he's feeling manly and primitive."

I had growled and kissed her and mauled her tiny ass in my hands pulling her hard to me. I was playing the fool. I had found that I could live on her laugh.

"Then maybe a little luxury, sporty model, something handmade and very expensive with a foreign sounding name and two seats and a convertible roof for when he's feeling suave and debonair and somewhat Cary Grant-ish."

I had kissed her again, more slowly this time, taking my time and letting my tongue explore her lips and mouth. I feather kissed her eyes and cheeks and released her. I had found that I could drink her kisses.

"Which are you today, right now?" she asked, her eyes glittering with a mischievous light like they always did when we were playing our bed games, before and after. "Are you feeling primitive or suave and debonair?"

"Tonight, sweetheart, I'm going to drive you like a truck."

I had rolled over on top of her and speared her, sinking to the hilt in one motion. She was always wet and ready for me. Always. She squealed like she always did. She wrapped her arms around my neck and her legs around my thighs and hooked me with her heels and pushed herself up at me as I pumped away hard and fast and deep.

"I love you in me, Douglas," she had breathed. "I think I love it more than anything in the world."

Everything went away. Everything became clear. I had found that I needed the touch of her skin more than I had ever needed sleep.

Once Sandy got comfortable with talking dirty, she was always saying stuff like that. It never failed to hasten me to the edge. She began to kiss me like a demon and I felt her start to react, start to squeeze and tug and cling and tease and pull at me like she always did just before she came.

I was pulled from my reverie by the buzzing of my cell phone. I checked the time in its little green screen. Four hours had passed. I don't know where I had been but it had been nice. It had been dark and quiet and Sandy had been there and it had been nice. I was hard as a rock. The little metal cough-drop box where I kept my blow was empty upside down on the floor by my feet. The brandy bottle, likewise empty, rolled beside it. My heart felt round and firm and heavy in my chest, like a softball left overnight in the rain or a cabbage. My head was light, empty. My septum was burning and swollen. My top lip was crusted and itchy with a trail of blood. Warren Zevon was long since finished. My legs were stiff and tingly from sitting half-naked on the bed. The briefcase was closed upside down beside me. I had a blackout, I thought. I've been staring at the wall for four hours. I'm cracking up. I will sit here and stare at the wall for the rest of my life.

It was Marjorie on the phone. I gave her a cautious 'hello'. I wasn't sure what my voice would do.

"Look Doug," she began without preamble. "I'm just going over the schedule for next week and I don't want to put any pressure on you what with a death in the family but it would sure help me out if I knew what your plans were your friend said you might want some time off and I can certainly understand that what with what I went through with my Dad last summer or was it two summers ago now."

Marjorie talked without thought or punctuation when she was being all official and managerial. We made fun of her behind her back. 'Death in the family', my friend had said. My head swam. I guess that was Reid or Carruthers calling me in sick or crazy from the diner. I thought I saw an answer. I thought I saw the way out. I thought I saw the solution which was to get the hell away from all of this, to marshal my thoughts. I would do what I had done for my whole life. I would run. I would hide. Like a wounded animal I would crawl off by myself to lick my wounds, to recover or to die.

"Yeah, Marj. I am going to have to take some personal time. Thanks for understanding. I'm going to need at least a week. Can you cover that?"

"Sure, Doug, that's no problem. You know how slow it is this early in the season can you call me middle of the week let me know what you want to do?"

She rang off. No problem, indeed. Not for good old Madge. I was out of her hair for a week. That was what her understanding had meant. I knew Alun and the other waiter hyenas would be growling and nipping around her as soon as she disconnected, looking to scoop the prime shifts and the prime sections my long tenure at the restaurant had earned me. She could buy a lot of good will and favour and collect valuable markers for herself by doling them out. Marjorie would not miss me. I had never kissed her ass like some of the others, didn't have to. I was a superstar. I could do no wrong. I was the owner's fair-haired boy. He let me get away with the drinking and being drunk on the job. He forgave the hangovers and the peppermint breath and the Visine-shiny eyes and the shortcuts and the paying of the bus staff to do my share of the side work because he knew I had it where it counted, at the tables, with the customers. I had never let him down there and had a long list of commendations to prove it. People demanded to sit in my section. People came back to his restaurant because of me. That was all that mattered to him. I had probably paid for most of his Hummer. I was his go-to guy and Marj hated that. She was the manager because she hadn't been able to handle the pace of the real work at the tables. She had tried and failed. She had been weighed in the balance and found wanting of the only thing that mattered. She had been promoted to keep her out of the way.

What would I do with my new-found week of freedom? I had to have a plan. My brain was racing but slow to work. I would definitely get out of town for a while. I was going to lose it sure as hell if I had to have another breakfast with the lawyers. I'd end up working alongside Dish at the High Times. I scooped all the stuff back into the briefcase, tossed in my cell and clicked it shut. Decided I could not manage a shower. Dressed. Slid downstairs to write a note on a chunk of paper towel for Christa.

'Family thing going on,' I wrote. 'Got to go away for

a while. I have my cell if you need me. Please don't be a lesbian when I get back. I have always loved you.'

A little trace of irreverent Douglas to ease her suspicions, not laid on too thick though. I knew to keep the volume down. God knows how many people she had told about the lawyers and what stories those people would be telling each other tonight at the bars and tomorrow at their liquid Monday lunch. I wondered what, if anything, I had ever said to them about family and what they were likely to remember. Didn't know. Didn't matter.

Back upstairs to pin the note to Christa's door. I contemplated calling The Belmont. No. I would call Siskel and Ebert from somewhere else that wasn't here, sometime that wasn't now. I did not trust myself. I wasn't sure what my voice would do. My stock of normal had been emptied during the exchange with Madge. Carrying the briefcase, I walked out the front door and turned left toward downtown. I thought briefly of taking a stroll down to the house on King's Landing. I thought again. No. Too soon. It might never be late enough to make that trip. I well knew the house the lawyers had said was now mine. I had been in it once every year for the past six or so, part of the catering crew that worked the opening night gala function. The owner of the house was a big-time retired lawyer who summered in our town and fancied himself an impresario of the arts. He gave enough to be named to the board of governors for the theatre company. I wondered where he was sleeping tonight. I wondered what my legal team had paid him to give up the most beautiful house in the world. You could just see the glimmer of its lights from Sandy's little balcony at The Belmont. I had told her all about it there later that first night. I had cradled her in my arms in front of me and tilted her head by the chin until she saw. I had whispered to her of the red, solid-looking, brick exterior and the fine crafted dark wood and leaded windows everywhere inside while I caressed the undersides of her breasts. I had told her of the perfect gardens and the infinity pool and the stainless-steel kitchen and the wine cellar and the patio lights and how the grounds sloped long and gentle down to a little dock and a boathouse on the river. I had told her about the library and how I longed to fill it with all the books I had ever loved but could only borrow from the library. I held her and told her how I would sit there each night in a leather armchair by the fire and read the classics if I only could. Pipe dreams. Stupid, silly wishes finally come true. All mine. All mine for the most terrible price.

"Hey, Douglas. Not working tonight? The town's hoppin', man."

It was Neil. He drove a local cab in the summer and skied the Rockies all winter and smoked black hash pretty much all of the time. In my narcotic haze he had slid silently up to the curb in his big, black Town Car.

"N'ah. I had a death in the family" I said after a while. "I'm off for a week or so. Can you give me a lift?"

"Sorry to hear that, brother. Where you headed?"

"I've got to get to the airport."

"Shit, Doug, that's 200 miles round trip. I'll miss the evening rush. And excuse me for sayin' so, but you look like you got a terrible load on, sure as shit. You sure you're up to flying."

Neil was ever the diplomat.

"How does five hundred bucks for the round-trip sound, my friend?"

I opened the briefcase on the trunk of his car and peeled off what I thought was $500 for him.

"For five hundred bucks, my brother, I am your bitch."

He popped the rear door locks and I got in. I saw just then for the first time how enough money could buy you anything and how comfortable I felt when buying it.

I don't remember much of the cab ride to the airport. I remember that Neil had a shoebox full of old John Lee Hooker cassette tapes and a kick-ass sound system on which to play them. I remember the bass throbbing and thrumming from the trunk like a massage. I remember he kept up a constant buzz and banter about the advantages and disadvantages of the several varieties of snow and about his mom and her cancer and some crazy Australian chick he had been banging through the winter. I remember half not listening. I remember not talking. I remember trails of strobey coloured lights and the Doppler noises of the highway. I remember passing some farmhouse with an out of this worldly glow and ghost horses and miles of bright white ghost fencing. I remember rolling by the white fence and the horses forever. I may have slept. All that other stuff might have been dreams.

*

Sandy returned from the bedroom wearing a little pinky silky robe that stopped about half way down her thighs. I offered her the drink I had prepared. She took a little sip. I could see the ghosts of her nipples, a shadow between her legs. She sat on the couch, knees Catholic schoolgirl prim together and patted the cushion beside her. I sat. We smiled.

"What are we drinking?"

"It's a Manhattan. Most people make them mostly rye with a little red vermouth. I like them mostly red vermouth with a little rye for kick and colour. You really should have some bitters and a cherry to make a good one but...."

I was babbling. The Stingers had taken charge. Booze made me a talker. Dope shut my mouth.

"Tasty," she said and smacked her lips. "I'm not usually much of a drinker. Not that you'd know that from the way I've been going at it tonight."

We were sitting beside each other, close, two sides of a little V. She had washed her face or splashed some water on it or some other tricksy, womanly thing. I could see tiny diamond beads at her forehead hair line and at her temple catching the light from the lamp beside us. I looked down at our legs, touching just barely at the knee. Mine, black wool tuxedo pants, a long stain of some creamy sauce splattered up my thigh. Hers, bare, pink, shining. I thought of alabaster. If alabaster is what I think it is, I'm looking at it, I thought. She began without further prologue.

"I was married when I was nineteen, Douglas."

My mind jumped to her at nineteen. If she was now what she was now, what must she have been at nineteen. The very thought made my breath catch a little hitch in my throat.

"I was a virgin."

My mind jumped. She put down her drink and squirmed around a little to face me more directly on the couch. Her pinky silky gown edged up her thighs. I tried not to stare. She sighed.

"Jesus. This is so hard."

She had no idea. I had lost my mind at the thought of Sandy, the nineteen-year-old virgin. She took a long breath and waded in again.

"I love my husband. I really do. He is a good and kind and gentle and decent man and he has always treated me like a queen. I went from my parents' house straight to his. I have never wanted for anything. Literally. My life could be a fairy tale."

She took a long breath. She took another Manhattan sip.

"It's sex, Douglas."

You betcha, I thought, it's always sex. I had known it was always sex since I had first known that there was sex. I said nothing. I had nothing more to say. I might never have anything more to say.

"I listen to my friends talking about sex, Douglas. They talk about things and feelings and sensations that I have never felt. I wonder if most men know the way that some women can go on about sex, as much as any man, maybe more. Most of my friends have had affairs and their husbands have too. They go on and on until I just can't bear it anymore. They all think I'm a big prude because I don't want to discuss my sex life or theirs for that matter in exquisite detail over a lunch salad. I let them think that. It makes it easier. I've had offers of course, usually crude, gropey propositions from my friends' husbands or my husband's friends when they've had too much to drink, but I've never taken anyone up on their offer. I just couldn't do that. But lately...."

She paused to refuel with Manhattan. She paused to breathe. I paused to breathe. I had forgotten about breathing.

"The only orgasms I've ever had are the ones I've given myself when I couldn't stand it anymore and I feel such guilt about those that they are few and far between."

I dared not think of that. She looked away. I was glad. Her constant gaze had a way of tearing me to pieces. I wanted to flee or take my own life, anything so that she could stop talking. Her words were killing me. I couldn't imagine what they were doing to her.

"My husband and I have been married for 25 years, Douglas, a quarter of a century, my whole adult life, and he's made love to me maybe 50 times and I wonder why. I have always been faithful and I keep myself in good shape. I am always available to him. I've never said no, never had a headache. I know that I am attractive to men. I try to please him in bed. I like to think that I'm a sensual woman...."

She started to blubber a bit now so I put down my empty glass and took her in my arms. She cried softly against my shoulder for a bit. Her pinky silky gown was cool and slippy under my fingers.

"On our anniversary this year," she whispered into my shoulder, "our 25th anniversary, he gave me a huge diamond pendant and he threw me a beautiful surprise party with all our friends but he didn't make love to me, Douglas. We said goodnight and we slept in our separate rooms. I'm sure it's because I'm not able to have children. I'm not right down there, for children."

She leaned back and gestured toward her torso with her chin and my eyes were drawn there. There! It was out of her. We were down to the short strokes. She clutched me again and her tears were a flood against my shirt, hot, they burned like acid.

"I think that he is not interested in me in that way, he hasn't been interested in me in that way for so long, since from the beginning maybe because I can't have children."

She was really letting it out now. I let her cry on.

"That's when I decided to find a man, that night after the anniversary party. I decided that I wasn't going to go through the rest of my life without experiencing some of what my friends are always going on about, some of what I read about in books and saw in the movies. I just wasn't. I always suspected they might be lying, exaggerating. I want to be sure. I want to see for myself. I want to be just a woman with just a man even if it's only once, even if it's just for a little while. I love my husband but I just have to know."

She pulled away and looked up into my face. Her eyes were blue liquid, miles deep. She had become determined. Her lashes were matted with tears. There was a shine under her nose. She had become more beautiful than I thought possible.

"….and then I found you, Douglas and I knew you were the one."

She smiled that smile again, the one that I would see every day for the rest of my life.

"I found you, so handsome and tall and slim, so silly, looking down the front of my dress and smiling with your beautiful dimples and showing off and messing up my order and acting so sweet and kind and helping me on with my sweater and I thought, he's the one. I knew it. He's the man I need. So sexy, so confident, so gallante. All my friends thought you were sweet on me. They teased me all night. They said the crudest things and all the teasing and the comments made me blush and tingle and the tingling helped me with my courage because I knew they were right. I felt it from the first time I saw you. I think you felt it too."

She gave me another one of those kisses, one small, cool, palm on either cheek, fingers up and around and behind the ears, nails digging slightly into my scalp. Her lips were like heaven and her tongue flattered mine.

"I suppose all you want now is to get the heck away from this crazy woman, don't you? Now that you know how messed up she is. I can't say I'd blame you."

What could I say to that, to the most beautiful woman I had ever been close to, the most beautiful woman to ever kiss me, a woman who tingled at the thought of silly, miserable me, what with her in a pinky, silky dressing gown and her perfect alabaster knee touching mine just so and burning a hole through my stained and wretched waiters' pants, a woman whose husband wouldn't fuck her when every other man in the world would have crawled over flaming, broken glass for just one of her smiles.

"Your friends were right, Sandy. I am sweet on you. I am so sweet on you I think I'm going to die. Would you like to dance?"

We smiled. I took her perfect hands in mine and stood and pulled her to her feet. Such were my dreams and, in my dreams, I was one hell of a slow dancer.

*

I became sentient again only when I stood, briefcase in hand, at the departures entrance to the airport. It was cool. I shivered and swayed. Neil tooted the horn, shave and a haircut, and drove away. I raised my hand in half-hearted salute and went inside and headed straight toward the neon sirens of the bar. I needed a Bloody Mary or 10. My thoughts were becoming dangerously clear. I was out of coke.

The bartender gave me a nervous look when I ordered my drink. I knew the look well. I had given it many times myself. It was the kind of look a person who sold liquor for a living gave to a red-eyed stranger, badly dressed, carrying a black briefcase clutched to his chest, who stumbled in to the bar at the end of the night and ordered a double and waited for it like an expectant first-time father. I ignored the bartender and his look, chugged the drink down, flipped him a twenty and escaped to the first ticket counter I saw.

"Yes, Sir. How can I help you this evening?"

She was bright-eyed and terribly young and pretty and very cheerful considering what she did for a living and the time of the night. The name tag on one substantial starched boob said 'Tammy' and told me she could speak English and French both.

I went to work. I was in self-preservation mode now, the self-preservation mode that gets you out of the fight brewing around you at the bar or away from the fat, possessive girl who's taken an unfortunate shine to you at last call for alcohol or gets you home when you're so drunk you can't think or dial the phone. I knew how I had to act if I was going to get away from the terrible darkness that threatened to engulf me. I had done it time and again before. I was Teflon. I was an eel. I flashed Tammy my best smile. I concentrated on forming words with my tongue. I concentrated on appearing benign, unremarkable, even pleasant. It was a stretch. My heart was coke pounding. My mouth was dry like sand. I thought I could feel a nasty facial tic involving my right eye.

"I'm looking for a quick getaway, Tammy. What's leaving tonight? Right now."

Tammy didn't even blink. Tammy was a pro. Tammy was an eel. Tammy had two languages. Tammy had seen it all. "Let's take a look, shall we?"

She turned to a computer monitor and began to quietly tap keys. Her tongue sneaked out a bit between her teeth as if to help her concentrate.

"We've got Sarasota. Oops, nope, sorry, that one just boarded."

She gave over an apologetic look like she had disappointed me in some fundamental way. She and the tip of her tongue and her two languages redoubled their efforts. I watched her brows furrow as she studied the screen. She was pretty but carrying a few extra pounds. They showed in her face. I felt confident this was going to turn out okay. She leaked competence. My problem was her problem now. I was with the good hands people.

"We've got a nice little charter to Las Vegas leaving – she consulted her tiny woman's watch – in about 15 minutes. You can just make it. How does that sound?"

She looked up at me all sweet and hopeful and competent.

"That's sounds perfect, Tammy."

It was. Vegas was just the ticket. I had been there a couple of years ago after the season for a long weekend stag party for a getting-married restaurant friend of mine. Nice hotels, good food and drink, lots of night-life, plenty of opportunity for me to stock up on the essential supplies I would need to weather this present storm, busy and crazy and anonymous enough that I could lose myself for as long as I needed to figure out some reasonable course of action. Opening the brief-case on the counter in front of her, I pushed past the neat, banded bundles of bills – a wad of cash for an airline ticket in my condition at that time of night was sure to get me noticed – and after a long, pregnant second of careful consideration handed her my virgin American Express card.

"Can I put it on that? I don't have but the one bag."

"Of course."

Her smile wavered just slightly as she looked from the card to my face to the card to my face but she bravely turned to her monitor and began to type. I figured that I was not the typical Amex black type of guy. I would have done the same double-take if some-one like me had presented me with such a card to pay for dinner. I turned away to face the tarmac windows as if I were terminally blasé, as if I had better things to do than watch someone type. Inside, my heart pound-ed away in its coke and liquor rhythm. What if the card was a fake?

("Mr. Edgars, the joke's on you!")

"Mr. Edgars!"

I spun toward her, more of a guilty, clumsy jerk of the body than a turn, a coke turn if there ever was one.

"First class, Sir?"

It took me an overly long moment to process the information. I hoped it looked as if I were considering things. I suspected that I just looked panicked. I made a snap decision. My last flight had been a red eye in coach with a bunch of drunken lunatics and drinks at $9.00 a pop and no leg room and one working bathroom for the whole cabin of us. My circumstances had changed and it looked like my new American Express had passed its first test.

"First class sounds just right for tonight. Thanks for suggesting it, Tammy."

She smiled, blushed, and turned again to resume typing; it sure did take a lot of typing to fly to Vegas. I glanced at the round, uplifted ass stretching the back of her blue skirt and fought back an urge like puking. God, how I had worshipped Sandy's delectable little ass, two unblemished handfuls, soft as sugar, none to waste.

"There we are. Done and done. Just sign here please, Mr. Edgars. We'd better rush. They've started to board."

I rushed and signed there and was pointed down a miles long corridor to the correct gate, there to be met by another beautiful phantom of a woman and ushered by her down a scary, shaky, windy little tunnel into a plush purple velveteen window seat in a row to myself and plied with champagne and food and hot towels and slippers and, before I knew it, I was standing outside the Las Vegas airport terminal, gripping my new briefcase under my arm like a football, safe landed and fed and drunk as a lord on domestic champagne and French cognac, and a pleasant looking black gentleman was asking if I needed a cab.

*

While Sandy had been in the bedroom doing her bedroom things, I had found an expensive-looking radio attached to an expensive-looking television console inside an expensive-looking armoire-type thing and tuned it to the local FM station. I knew my friend Paul would be spinning the tunes that night late and I knew that he liked the same music I did. He would probably be righteously baked, his feet up on the console, playing album sides and keeping the chatter to a minimum.

When I pulled Sandy gently to her feet and manoeuvred her to the little carpeted area between the sofa and the bedroom door, Paul was just introducing the Side One of the first Counting Crows album. I took this as an omen of good karma. I usually didn't like dancing, hated it actually, thought it a pointless waste of time. But I knew it served its purpose every now and again and the only such purpose was getting close to a beautiful woman you wanted to go to bed with but to whom you did not know what to say next. So, we danced. She seemed content to cling to me like that for a while. I was content to cling to her like that for the rest of my life. Her cheek was against my chest. My chin was nestled in her hair. Her hair smelt like candy. I held one of her hands in mine clutched to my left shoulder but high so she wouldn't feel my overbeating heart. I pressed my other hand feather gently against her lower back. Her free arm was loose around me and she was making these crazy looping movements between my shoulder blades with the tips of her fingers. I was sweating like all get out. She felt cool as spring. She smelled like morning in heaven. Between us my cock pushed unabashedly rigid against her pelvis. Our shuffling feet on the carpet were as loud as the music. When I could bear it no longer, I pushed her gently away until I could see into her eyes. I raised my palm to her cheek and touched her softly there.

"Someone should be making love to you every night, Sandy," I began. "You are the most beautiful woman I've ever seen. You're vibrant and sexy and so full of life. You're smart and funny and drop dead gorgeous and the best kisser in the world. I'm so nervous right now....I haven't felt this way since the night of my senior prom. Oh shit, I'm babbling like a schoolboy idiot now. I didn't even go to my high school prom. You're going to chase me out of here, or I'm going to run."

My voice faded out. I pulled her to me and pressed my lips to her hair, just resting, regrouping.

"You're doing perfectly, Douglas," she whispered, pushing against my chest again until we were far enough apart for her to fix me again with those eyes. "You're doing perfectly. Tell me again about the beautiful part and the sexy and the vibrant and the kissing and the gorgeous."

I took a deep breath preparing to start again but before the advance had even started I began to beat my hasty retreat. Doubt had rushed in. Such things as this did not happen to guys like me. Women like Sandy didn't fall into men's laps. They certainly didn't fall into mine. Women like Sandy didn't give me the time of day. I was invisible to them. I was not worthy. This had been a bad idea from the start. What the hell had I been thinking? I wondered if I could still make last call at Bentley's. I looked for the out.

"The truth is, Sandy, I'm not sure if we want the same things here. I want you so very much. Hell, every man who sees you wants you. But, to be honest, I'm a bit afraid of the responsibility. I mean, you're talking here about your husband and children and....you're looking for love making and bucket list life experience stuff and I'm not all that confident in my abilities right now or ever, for that matter. I'm a quick roll in the hay type of guy. You're like some sort of fucking princess but I'm nobody's prince. You're my dream girl and my dreams don't usually come true. I think I'm going to wake up any minute now and I'm going to be terribly pissed off."

I was babbling. I pulled her to me. I wanted to hide. I wanted to disappear. I was the lion caught out in his lies. They were on to me. That bitch Dorothy had called my bluff, threatened to kick my ass, and I was on the run. Sandy thought different. Sandy pushed away again and ran her palm down my cheek and rested it on my chest. It burned there.

"You're wrong, Douglas."

She kissed me. Soft.

"I know you're the right man."

She kissed me again. Hard.

"I know you're the right man because I wanted you to look down my dress at the restaurant tonight. I pushed my chest out at you every chance I got. I never did that before, never wanted too. And you know what else? It felt good and right. I know you're the right man because I love the way you smell like a man and the way your kisses go right through me and because you kissed me in the stairwell and, if you'd wanted, I would have given myself to you right there on the stairs."

She kissed me once more. Soft.

"I've been made love to before, Douglas. I want more than that once in my life, or twice, or three times. It's that simple. It's got to be you. It's out of our hands now, don't you think."

She kissed me then, hard, and we were lying on the bed on top of a musty-smelling, satiny quilted cover in the dark, and we were kissing deeper and longer and harder than any two people had ever kissed before, and my palm was suddenly on the swell of her naked hip and my fingers were inexplicably gripping her ass as she lay facing me, and as she rolled away my fingers were just barely touching the first cut of her pubic hair, warm and soft and crispy like rice paper, and I could feel her insistent little fingers tugging like puppies at the stupid, stubborn buttons of my shirt.

*

"Where can I take you, Sir? You got a reservation somewheres?"

The pleasant looking black gentleman reached for the briefcase and I came to. I waved him off the briefcase and got into the back seat of the cab.

"Where to, Sir?"

His smile was becoming a little thin and nervous. I knew I had to act fast.

"No reservations, no. This trip was spur of the moment. I just had to get away for a little R and R, you know."

I gave him my best tired brother needs a little R and R grin. Just the two of us friends against the world.

"I'm looking to blow off some steam for a couple of days, maybe a week. Where's the best place for that? Where do you think I should be?"

"Just two questions I got to ask in that regards, Sir. Number one, you got a heavy wallet?"

He had relaxed now that we were down to the brass tacks of his business.

"No problems there, my friend. My wallet's so heavy these days I can barely lift it."

If he only knew.

"Excellent." He pronounced it egg-saalaad and I loved him for it.

"Question number two is whats kind a man you is. You the kind wants the lights and the brights and the big shows and the expensive dinners that don't fill you up none and all the best write-ups in all the airplane magazines and you end up payin' a short ton for a little room looks out over the back-alley garbage can? Or you the kind wants to trust Chester and go to the bestest of the best where they know what it is a man needs to relax his own self?"

I loved this Chester man even more. He was reading my mind.

"Chester, I want to go to where the Queen of England would stay if she came to Vegas on the sly to play some craps and get a load on."

We laughed together, Chester and I.

"Right you is, Mister. The Queen of England you is."

We drove off with Chester making non-stop chatter about the sights and sounds and who was playing in town and who was staying in town and what we were seeing on our left and our right. After a short twenty minutes he pulled off the street and under a rich purple canopy. Before the car had rolled to a stop the car door was yanked open by another uniformed black man.

"That'll be $14.50."

Chester read off the meter to me. I pressed two of my endless hundreds into his hand and said thanks. He looked from the money to me.

"Mister, you ever need a cab ride in this old town, you ask the concierge here, Mr. King, to get hold of ol' Chester. He got my number. He got everybody's number. Mr. King, he got everything."

I shook his hand.

"My name is Douglas," I said, "and you are my driver but I don't know if I'll be travelling much. One thing though Chester, where are we? What's the name of this hotel?"

"This ain't no hotel, Mr. Douglas. This here's The

Taitinger. The Taitinger ain't just no hotel. It just is what it is. You'll see."

He drove off with a squeak of the tires. I followed the second black gentleman up a short flight of stairs. Marble, I think. Some sort of stone for sure. The soles of my shoes rang off them with soft little slaps.

*

Sandy and I kissed on the bed for the longest time. I would have been content to kiss her on the bed for the rest of my life. Her lips were food to me. We would go full bore, tongue battling tongue for a bit and then draw back for little nips and smacks and licks and then she would be on my face and eyes and I would be on hers and then we would be back at it, tongue to lashing tongue. Our hands were mauling each others' bodies. Her nightie thing let go with a loud rip. We gasped and laughed and pressed on.

At some point we managed to get my pants and boxers off, her pushing, me twitching, pantlegs inside out, a handful of change spilling to the bed. At some point she was astride me and I was buried instantly inside her. She moaned just then like she was dying and she smiled like she had been shot She threw her head back and gasped and I loved her at that moment, loved her with all the love in the world. Her breasts, unfettered, were even better than I had imagined. Full and lush and heavy. Magical. Her wrinkled pink nipples looked ready to pop. She moaned as I pulled at them and smiled and her smile told me that I was the right man after all. I was the perfect man. She moaned a deep, throaty moan and she grimaced with concentration and leaned down to kiss me and I felt her slide over and around me like a firm hand holding a satin swatch soaked with hot oil and I was closer to heaven than I've ever been. She moaned and she kissed me and then, pushing off my chest with both palms flat, she sat up and pulled the remnant of her pinky silky robe over her shoulders and tossed it to the floor and leaned toward me again. I filled my hands with her breasts, pulling and kneading like they were my first. She moaned another moan and grabbed my wrists, pulling my hands tighter to her, her hands urging mine to squeeze harder. Leaning again toward me, she whispered into my ear;

"You're the one, Douglas. No question about it."

She caught the flesh of an ear in her mouth and bit gently. We began to bounce and thrust and roll in earnest and heaven, which once I thought so near, came rushing toward me from a tremendous distance at some unfathomable speed.

*

Checking in out of nowhere in the middle of the night proved to be a challenge, even in the city that never sleeps, even at Chester's fabled Taitinger. At least it was for a newly insane, bedraggled, half-drunken, coke hungover stranger with a briefcase full of money and an attitude. Halfway between Chester and the front desk, halfway up the stony steps, I had decided with crystal-clear cocaine logic that I deserved to be living in the lap of luxury here at The Taitinger. The very name rolled off my tongue. I was entitled. The lobby made The Belmont look like a barn. This was where I was meant to be. This was the least the world could do to right the terrible wrong inflicted upon me.

I started at obnoxious. I started at B-movie crass. I started badly. I started in a loud voice. I told the clerk at the desk that I wanted the penthouse suite and, when told that it was not available, I became indignant and shrill. There were just three of us in the sumptuous lobby. Me, across a heavy wood counter from a hapless, young clerk. The door man was huddled nervously nearby. I can see now that I was being petulant and stupid. I was a toddler hearing 'no' for the first time since I had received my magic satchel of greenbacks. I was flashing Benjamins around like a drunken waiter – sailors got nothing on us – and making barely coherent promises and threats when I felt a firm hand land on my shoulder and run down my arm, gripping, effectively pinning me to the counter. The owner of the firm hand was of medium height and slight build but with one glance at his face I was aware of great strength. For a moment I was afraid.

"I'm Mr. King. I'm the concierge. Can I help in any way?"

He looked directly into my eyes and then up me and down me and through me and all around and then to the eyes again. In a second or two, I knew he had taken my entire sorry inventory and arrived at a sad conclusion. He had taken the measure of me. I had spent a lifetime in service. I knew my betters. I knew when to retreat. I back-pedalled and came around again.

"I just want a suite for the night and – a glance at the clerk's name tag – Gary here won't give me one."

My voice was whiny. In my hand I clutched a sweaty wrinkle of bills. I had never felt so stupid.

"That's not what I heard, Sir. What I heard was you demanding the penthouse suite from Gary and Gary doing his best to politely and diplomatically tell you that the penthouse suite is occupied and trying to interest you in one of our other splendid rooms. Here at The Taitinger we are not in the habit of evicting our sleeping guests from their rooms in the middle of the night just because someone comes in and shakes a pile of money at us. That wouldn't be good for business, now would it?"

He smiled now but the smile was grim and his voice was just a step back from the edge. There was anger there too. There was a feeling that he had taken my boorish behaviour as a personal affront. Somehow during our exchange, he had managed to manoeuvre me to one side of the lobby. The door man had melted back to his door man duties and Gary had become busy, busy at a computer terminal.

We were all alone, Mr. King and I. My first five minutes might never have happened. The Taitinger lobby was quiet. We were just two old pals having a quiet chat.

"Now here's what's going to happen Mr...?"

I fed him my name. I was a kid with the principal. I

was a person of interest. I was under the lights. I was an unindicted co-conspirator.

"Now here's what's going to happen, Mr. Edgars. That is, if you really want to stay with us at The Taitinger and I sincerely hope you do. I think that you are Taitinger material, at least you are a couple of layers down. We're going to go back up to the front desk. You're going to offer Gary your apologies for your actions and your tone and ask for the best room he's got available. You're definitely going to keep that cash hidden away because flashing that much cash can get you killed quick in Las Vegas or most other places. Then I'm going to take you up to your room and you're going to get a good night's sleep. I can smell your need for a good night's sleep, Mr. Edgars. Have we reached an understanding?"

I assured him that we had. I was beat. I was a shoplifting kid collared by the store detective. I was the cowed husband caught sneaking in late. It went exactly like he said it would. I pocketed the cash and gave Gary my Amex. I signed the necessary papers. Gary wished me a pleasant stay. Mr. King led me to the elevator and to my suite in an elegant silence. He swiped my key card and ushered me into the room. He turned on the lights and explained how to operate the television and heating and the bathroom hot tub and explained the hours for maid service and mentioned the 24-hour room service and wished me a good night and a good stay. Through this, I stood in the centre of the living room like a slack-jawed rube. As he left he snapped his card down on a little table near the door and smiled with an uncertain warmth.

"I am Mr. King. I am the concierge of this beautiful hotel and that means I do for the guests. The number on the card rings in my pocket any time, day or night. Please don't hesitate to call but please leave the attitude I saw in the lobby in your pocket, Mr. Edgars. It does not fit in here at The Taitinger. I look forward to getting to know you better. I look forward to making your stay here a truly pleasant one. You look to me, if I may presume, like someone who could use a pleasant stay, a pleasant something."

What I heard was 'Here's your second chance; fuck over me or the staff again boyo and you're out on your ear'. I accepted that as my due. I was the late-night, front-porch suitor caught with his hand up the church social daughter's shirt. He left. Chastened, I found a split of champagne in the mini-bar fridge, chugged it down, and fell into bed.

I woke much later with the lights full on, still in my clothes, feeling like home-made shit. Coke always ate me up the next day. The sun blazed in an enormous window. Outside, below, the buildings of the Vegas strip danced in a shimmer of heat. Inside the Taitinger, inside my room, it was quiet and still. I went to the bathroom and pissed like a race horse. Everything was marble. I drained another couple of mini-bottles, washed them down with water from the tap, and went back to bed. The bed was big as an airport departure lounge and perfectly soft.

*

After a bit, Sandy reared back and jolted herself down into my pelvis and held us there. She thrashed her head back and forth, flinging her hair like a headbanger metal fan. I watched in wonder, in awe, as she bit that beautiful bottom lip in unmistakeable climax. I followed a long second later and then she was in my arms, her full weight collapsed on me like she had fainted. My hands were running slowly up and down her moist back as she heaved and panted into the hair on my chest. We rested.

"Oh, Douglas."

She lifted her head after a long while, raised up to her elbows, smiled hard with her eyes, and kissed me rough on the mouth.

"Am I crushing you, sweetheart?"

I assured her that she was as light as a feather and that I had never been happier nor more comfortable in my life nor would I ever be again. She pushed up to a sitting position and I watched a bead of sweat run down the valley between her breasts. I reached for it with my tongue.

"You did it. You really did it."

She was laughing now, giddy and dangerously beautiful. Powerful. Complete. A force of nature. I knew that I would hurl myself through the window glass if she were to only ask. She treated me to more of her tongue. Her tongue had become my favourite thing in the world.

"You did it, Douglas. I had one, an orgasm. I'm sure

of it. A beautiful monster curl-your-toes just like in the trashy novels orgasm. I really thought I was going to explode or maybe die but I never wanted it to end."

She looked so proud and perfect, her smile looked about to split her face. She was the most beautiful thing on the planet. She was a little girl who had just ridden a two-wheeler for the first time.

"And you know what else? I want more of them. I have some catching up to do."

"I didn't really do anything, Sandy. I was just lying here with a hard-on. You did it. You did all the work. You did it for both of us and you did it very nicely indeed."

"I did, didn't I?"

She seemed embarrassed but pleased. I sat up until her legs were wrapped around my hips behind me. I felt her muscles shift and clutch at me and I was instantly hard again.

"You most certainly did. You were wonderful. You are wonderful."

I kissed her hard and, grabbing her about the waist, pushed her deeper onto me. I was a teenager again, a stallion. I would never go soft.

"I want you again, Sandy. I want you again and again. Let me do all the work this time. I want you to enjoy this one right from the beginning."

Rolling her onto her back, I pushed into her and felt her grip me. I fucked her as best I could, as best as I knew how. I fucked her and kissed her and sucked and bit her breasts and nipples and roamed my hands over the exquisite silk of her body, pausing here to pinch her clitoris and there to probe her clutching anus. I lifted her legs to her shoulders and held them there while I pumped like a dynamo. I let them slide to her sides while I stroked deep and slow. Always the kissing. I laughed at her when she came again. I whispered in her ear that she was my woman and my angel. I shouted to her how tight she was, how hot and oily. I asked her to beg for it harder and when she did I stopped and worked her nipples for a while. When she begged me to stop I pounded on all that much harder. When I came the second time I lifted her off the bed and she raked my back and bit my shoulder and urged me on and we went even higher. Finally, I could take no more. I rolled off, too sensitive for another touch.

Even then, sated, I could not bear the lost contact. I rolled back toward her and taking her in my hands, crushed her toward me and buried my face in the soft pillows of her breasts. Her hands worked my hair as we panted in unison. I tried to work my way toward her fast beating heart with my lips and teeth and tongue.

*

I came awake the second time slow and took my bearings even slower. I looked around me and knew I was in Vegas. I knew how I had come to be there. I remembered why. I could smell myself; the stale, acrid acid sweat of another coke and booze bender just over. It disgusted me. Stripping off my clothes, I went to the bathroom and took a hot shower, then a cold, and then another hot. The shower had jets that came from the top and the sides both. I stayed in there a long time. There were big puffy towels like blankets and then I was back to the bedroom to dress.

No clothes. In my insane cocaine haste, I had packed the money and the yellow envelopes into that single sorry briefcase and come away without a change of clothes or even a toothbrush. I thought for a moment, naked on the bed, and reached for Mr. King's card and the telephone. He had said that he was there to do for his guests. Well, I certainly needed doing for. He answered on the first ring. I hadn't even glanced at the time. Outside it was dusky, late in the day, or maybe early.

"Julius King, how can I help you?"

His voice was smooth and melodious and calming, just as I remembered it.

"Mr. King, this is Doug Edgars. You remember me? I checked in so charmingly last night."

I was contrite and ashamed although I had done far worse before without thinking of apologizing.

"Of course, Mr. Edgars. I trust that you're comfortable. Did you sleep well?"

I assured him that I was and that I had, although comfortable was the last word I would have used to describe myself at that point of my life. We came to the end of the small talk.

"How can The Taitinger help you today, Mr. Edgars?"

I explained to him that I had come away without the appropriate clothes for the season in Las Vegas and needed some help to buy some. He just chuckled.

"That's an easy one, Mr. Edgar. As you may have heard, people sometimes lose their shirts here in Las Vegas and need help to have them replaced. I'll send a shopper up to your room in about a half-hour. Just tell her what you need and your sizes and preferences and the like and she'll do you proud. Anything else I can do for you this afternoon?"

So, it was afternoon. I wondered of which day.

"Not at the moment," I assured him, and made ready to ring off.

"Mr. Edgars, I was hoping that you'd give me a moment of your time later today. Say around six. We got off on a funny foot when you checked in. I'd like to put that to right."

We made arrangements for my room at six and said goodbye. 'You sometimes get a second chance to make a first impression,' he had said after my clumsy apology. Funny, my aunt used to say the same thing.

*

"I still have my socks on," I laughed as Sandy and I spiralled down from our high. I felt drunk. I felt the perfect glow that I remembered feeling after my first glass of champagne, the perfect ease and comfort of a clueless fifteen-year-old with a pocket full of drunken tip money and a belly full of bubbles after a lucrative New Year's Eve shift. Sandy was curled toward me now, my right arm around and behind her, her face pulled toward me where my shoulder met my neck. She purred a little guttural sound and ground her face deeper into me. Her right hand was drawing pictures on my chest. I felt an urgent need to take my socks off and an even more urgent need not to disturb this angel on my arm. We rested.

*

Mr. King's shopper had been and gone like a miracle when he knocked on my door promptly at 6:00. Her name was Nancy. She was a frumpy and severe woman of about seventy with a very business-like demeanour. She had measured me up and down and all around and asked about a hundred questions about styles and colours and budget and lifestyle and activities and then bustled off. She was back in two hours with two young men she introduced as her grandsons. The grandsons were heavily laden with boxes and bags. Neither looked much like Nancy. One was quite black. The service extended to clothing and care education and the putting away of things in closets and drawers. While Nancy narrated, the grandsons had pulled items from bags and boxes, held them up for my cursory inspection, removed tags and labels and then neatly folded them and put them away. When they left, my head was swimming with colour combinations and a million tips on care and handling and my closet and dresser drawers were pretty much full.

"How do I pay you for all this. How much did it all cost" I had asked as they began to say their goodbyes?

"It will all be added to your bill here," Nancy assured me. "The Taitinger has arrangements with all the best shops."

"How do you get paid," I persisted?

"My time and that of the boys will be added to the bill too and we ain't cheap," she smiled. "Of course, we're none of us adverse to a more tangible type show of gratitude if you liked the service."

I tipped Nancy a thousand bucks and her two grandsons two bills each. When Mr. King knocked on the door, I was dressed in new khakis and moccasins and silk underwear and a silk shirt and vest. I was looking so good I was thinking about a haircut. I was sure I had never looked better. I had never worn silk anything before. I had never worn moccasins.

*

Mr. King was younger than I remembered from our previous abbreviated meeting. He was stocky in build, medium height, hair thick and prematurely grey. He was impeccably dressed and I wondered if Nancy shopped for him too. He was a little on the short side but he looked like he could handle himself. I wondered if he had ever boxed. He looked the type. He had hands like hams.

I ushered him in and sat him down and offered him a drink. I had rediscovered the joys of the mini-bar. I was on my third imported beer and my second packet of nuts.

"I don't drink on the job, Mr. Edgars, and I'm always on the job."

He accepted a can of Diet Coke. I brought it to him and we sat opposite each other on two facing couches. The suite's living room seemed to be about twenty times the size of my room back home and had ten times the furniture. Like Sandy's had been, my bedroom with its stench and its rumpled covers were hidden behind a closed door. I asked the obvious question.

"I work for The Taitinger, Mr. Edgars. The biggest part of my job is to get things for our guests, to meet their needs, whatever their needs might be."

He paused, looking around as if he liked what I had done with the place.

"I am called the concierge, and to be the concierge of an institution like The Taitinger in a city like Las Vegas carries a certain prestige and a certain responsibility."

He paused to take a long, slow sip. Pulling a slim gold case from his breast pocket, he asked if I minded if he smoked. I said no, and bummed one myself. He lit both with a very utilitarian battered brass Zippo and, as if knowing our conversation would be a long one, left the cigarettes and lighter on the table between us. He gestured a 'help yourself' gesture with his chin.

"Part of my job is also to look after The Taitinger, Mr. Edgars", he continued, "and make sure no harm comes to her. This hotel has been my home for a long while. I love it almost like a man loves a woman. More maybe, for The Taitinger has never let me down. For that reason, I have vowed to never let her down."

We pondered the terrible implications of that statement. Another sip of Diet Coke. A swallow of beer. A flick of cigarette ash.

"It's none of my business of course, Mr. Edgars, but when a man checks into my hotel in the middle of the night in an agitated state and starts waving around handfuls of long green....well I start to wonder. The owner of the hotel pays me to wonder about things like that. He's a very private, very careful man and he expects me to be private and careful."

When he said agitated, I heard drunk and stoned and stupid. I felt foolish and embarrassed. My thoughts went to what exactly had landed me in Mr. King's front yard and, by the time we were done our talking, I had told him the whole story and his cigarettes were gone and we had called room service for another carton and bring some more beers and Diet Coke while you're at it. With Mr. King there was no lying and no hedging and no avoiding the unpleasant. Mr. King was a truth serum. For the first time in my life, I told another human being the whole truth the first time around and was happy to do it. I might have cried a little but it all came out. He listened to the whole story right through to the end without once flinching. I got the impression he was a difficult man to shock and an impossible one to surprise.

*

Sandy and I came alive together. She stirred. I rose to one elbow to gaze down at her. She opened her eyes slowly and blinked a bit at the light. For the first of many times with her, I chastised myself. How dare I not have considered how the harsh light would hurt her eyes? This was a new thing for me. I had been on my own for a long time and always considered my own comfort first and usually second and third too. I was a selfish man. It was a shortcoming I realized but could not hope to change. I had been on my own for a very long time and was a firm proponent of the dictum, 'God helps those who help themselves'. With Sandy, for the first time in my adult life, perhaps ever, for the first time that I wasn't being paid to do so, I put someone else's comfort before my own. It was like an instinct. I reached over and switched off the bedside lamp. That left us on the edge of a splash of light coming through the open door of the sitting room. It spilled up Sandy's legs, tangling in her dusting of pubic hair, and coming to rest in her eyelashes. I peeled off my socks and tossed them to the floor near my pants. I turned toward her and kissed her softly.

"You might be right. It felt like I was the right man, Sandy. It felt like I was the perfect man for that job."

I smiled down at her. It felt foreign for my face had forgotten what it felt like to smile and mean it.

"It certainly did, Douglas. It most certainly did."

She sighed and smiled and drew my face to hers and kissed me again better than she had ever kissed me before. She was smiling up at me and her face was shining like a star. One warm, soft breast lolled against my arm, her thigh pushed mine. I felt my cock stir. I leaned in. She leaned away.

"You're dripping out of me, sweetheart. Excuse me, will you, while I go and freshen up."

None of my dates had ever said that before. She pushed up and looked around for her clothes. I felt something like panic.

"Don't put anything on Sandy please, just hurry back."

She looked guilty and nervous and awkward but she complied. As she slipped off the bed, I cupped and squeezed her right breast which was even more perfect than the left to my eye, fuller and slightly more proud. With her gone, I slipped out of bed myself and went to my own whore's bath; washing my cock and balls and brushing and mouth washing with the complimentary supplies in the second bathroom. We arrived back to the bedroom at the same moment and I gathered her to me as if we had been separated by the long years of some war.

*

When I was done telling my story to Mr. King there was a long silence, long enough for me to become embarrassed in front of my confessor. I hedged.

"I'm sure you have somewhere to be, Mr. King. I'd understand if you had to leave and do your thing."

"I am doing my thing, Mr. Edgars. I'm getting to know the guests of my hotel. I have enjoyed getting to know you. I enjoyed your story. At first glance, I thought you were probably the idle son of some rich father, fleeing some unfortunate situation, a pregnant girlfriend perhaps. All that cash made me think for a moment that there was some crime involved. You have provided a much more interesting and satisfying tale."

He chugged the remainder of his drink. "It's eight now, Mr. Edgars. I usually eat dinner at ten. Will you join me? I'll be in the dining room on the third floor."

Shaking my hand firmly, he left. I was left wondering how I could have opened my heart and soul in such a manner to a man I did not know and wondering why it had felt so good and why I had not done it before. My heart had been too full.

*

Sandy had taken a quick shower. The wispy hairs at the base of her neck were limp and moist against her shoulders. Still, that scent surrounded her. It's her, I thought. It's not some perfume or hair spray. That smell just exudes from her pores. It's the smell of a beautiful women. She sweats it.

Grasping her ass in my palms, I lifted her to me and loved the way she squealed and nestled against me, her arms tight, tight around my neck. I was hard again. I laid her gently on the bed. The tips of her toes, polished with clear polish, just touching the floor. I loved that she was small. Kneeling before her, I leaned in to kiss her and then gently pushed her back to our bed, still relatively undisturbed. I ran my hands down each thigh to each ankle and gripping her there, raised them until her feet were flat on the bed. I leaned in. Our sex and her shower had parted her lips and they glistened in front of me, pink with hints and shadows of paler and darker pink within. I kissed her there. Her hands worked nervous in my hair.

"You don't have to do that, Douglas."

Her voice was wavering, thin, uncertain.

"I want to do this, Sandy. I want to do this more than anything in the whole world right now."

I leaned into her and felt her most intimate flesh on my lips, moist, sweet, sticky. I pushed my face into her and breathed deep.

*

There was a night long ago in the desert of years that immediately followed university. I was finished with school. I had no urge, no drive, no motivation, to find a career. I took a job. By default, that job was back in the restaurant trade. I began working at a private golf club way off from the city. I was a dining room captain, a head waiter, a boss of sorts but very much one of the boys. Truth is, there were very few others to boss had I been so inclined. We were a small crew and we all did it all. The only difference between me and the waiters was that I wore a tuxedo. I made an obscene amount of money to de-bone duck and Dover sole and prepare Caesar salad and *crepes Suzette* tableside for the idle rich. Most evenings, I just wandered from table to table, from dining room to lounge, glad handing, asking the men about their golf games and telling the ladies that they looked young and thin and wonderful. With my wage and cash tips I made as much as some doctors. I spent like nobody's business. I saved nothing at all for a rainy day.

There were six of us who lived on the club's third floor during the busy summer season because the buses did not travel to the outskirts and we couldn't make it to work on time. The course closed at dusk and opened early for the dawn golfing crowd. We served dinner, cleaned up the mess, and turned it all around for breakfast the next day. Two cooks, the captain, an assistant from the pro shop, and two waiters, three boys and three girls, all single, all rootless, all between nineteen and thirty. The parties were legendary. The late nights were legion.

The six of us dropped acid one night after dinner service and decided to walk the golf course in the dark. Outside it was warm and wet and foggy and enchanted. A thick mist overtook us as we walked down the gentle hill from the clubhouse to the 1st fairway; up to our ankles first, then our waists, our necks, and then, all in a swirl, it was in our eyes and ears and hair and we were confused and blind and giddy and scared. Then, just as suddenly, we were beyond it and below it and it floated like a crisp and freshly laundered bed sheet above us.

I remembered the sensation of magic. I remembered purity. I remembered stumbling and following some one, some leader who did not know the way. I remembered stumbling on a root or a rock or a dip and falling slowly, slowly into the side-hill path. I lay there, my face buried in soft, dewy soil. I had to lie there. I had been chosen to lie there. I would have lain there for the rest of my life had not my companions picked me up and sat me down and propped me up and dusted me off and offered me a drink from the supply we carried. (It was Tom Collins for me that night. I had the keys to the kingdom. I was the conspirator who had stolen the fixings from the house bar and carefully prepared a gallon bottle supply for each of the walk's participants. Tom Collins for me, some sort of ersatz daiquiri for Betty, an enormous screwdriver for Steve, a 12-pack of Miller Lite for Cathy who drank only beer. I forget what all else.) Sitting there in the dirt at the side of the path with Tom Collins dripping down my shirt and pants and pouring down my opened throat, with my friends all round me laughing and carrying on, all I wanted at that moment was to push my face back into the earth and taste its musty iron flavour. I remembered shrieking at the top of my lungs from the sheer joy and lust and confusion and abandon of it all and how my shrieking had alarmed the group and scared them, how it scared and alarmed me. I remembered Steve Collingwood, my best friend of that moment, dead now of AIDS which had gone through the hospitality industry like a scythe in the eighties, flopping down beside me, taking me in his arms and hugging me to him and saying close to my ear;

"Come on, Douglas. You're freakin' out and you're freakin' everybody else out. It's just the drugs, man. It's just the acid got hold of your brain. You know that. You been there before. It will all be alright."

The alive Steve had been that way. He was always the voice of reason in the most unreasonable of circumstance. He is that way still, in heaven, I am sure. He could be no other way. It was not in his nature. I understood what he was saying and what I wanted to say at the time was...

"No, Stevie, it's not the drugs this time. It's not the booze. It's the earth. It's the earth. I was eating the earth and it was delicious and it was giving me life."

...but our thoughts and our lives were moving too quickly on that evening and the thought slipped my mind and time moved us on. It slipped my mind until I leaned into the very centre of Sandy on the edge of that bed in The Belmont and took life from her.

I loved her there carefully. I loved her there not for her but for me. I explored her from knee to thigh, from knee to thigh. I let my tongue drift down low toward her ass and played with her there. I fluttered and I teased and I tormented the lips and the clit. I heard her lusty, anxious, approving noises begin. I buried myself in her, sucking the vulva into my mouth and nipping and biting them. I stuck my tongue in the hole from which she had given me such pleasure and felt it tense and clutch. When I felt her fingers in my hair tighten to the painful and felt her feet on my shoulders spasm and thump, I went for her clit and sucked it to me and beat it with my tongue until I was faint. I felt her thrashing. I pinned her to the bed with my fore-arms and shoulders and felt her gasp and pivot. She was a bronco and I, the rider. We calmed. I let her feel my tongue, slow now, gentle, swipe by little swipe, enjoying the way it made her shiver and jump and quiver. We came to a mutual *entente*. I pulled her to me until the wetness of her was pressed hard against my neck and my head was resting on her belly. I flicked my tongue lazily at her navel. She stroked my hair with her fingers. She ran the soles of her feet back and forth across my back. In the background there was some soft, discordant, and completely beautiful kind of music.

*

At ten, I found Mr. King at a table behind a bit of a screen toward the rear of the hotel's signature dining room. He was reading the newspaper.

"Oh, there you are. Just in time. Perfect. I'm famished. I missed lunch somehow."

He put away the paper and we got down to the business of dinner. I was familiar with the waiter's behaviour. Our fellow, whose name was Franz, was nervous to the point of apoplexy despite the fact that we were the easiest table in the world; two soups and two swordfish specials. Mr. King was sipping what looked to be a fizzy sort of lemonade. I ordered a double Manhattan up while we waited and asked Franz to pick out a nice half bottle of wine for my fish. He scurried off to the kitchen as if he had just been told his family would be spared the noose.

I asked Mr. King how his day was going and he said just fine. He asked how my day was going. I told him about losing seven hundred dollars to the slots on the way to the dining room. He smiled and said he didn't gamble when he was working and he was working all the time. When my drink arrived, we clinked glasses and I asked him, straight up, to tell me a little about himself and he did.

He told me the high and low lights of an impoverished childhood on the shore without a father and the fights in school because of his drunken mom. He told me about quitting school young and about his slow rise up the service ladder, from the dish pit of a clam shack on the beach to the prep kitchen to the dining room, from one restaurant to the next, each one a little higher up the scale, until the night he had served the owner of The Taitinger at an Atlantic City steakhouse and impressed him to the point where the owner had followed up with a job offer and a plane ticket to Vegas and a job in the hotel dining room that would eventually lead to where he was now. He had been 22 years old when he came to Las Vegas and, before then, had never before been more than 20 minutes from the hospital where he'd been born.

Over soup he told me some of the things he had seen and done since, the celebrities – without mentioning names, for Mr. King was the soul of discretion – he had serviced and the things he had provided, the hookers and the drugs and the specialties.

"So, if I'm staying at The Taitinger and I need or want something, it's your job to try to get it for me?" I asked, innocent as a lamb.

"Within the bounds of human decency and the Nevada criminal code," he laughed. "And even that last bit doesn't necessarily stop us at The Taitinger. We don't hold for punishing people for victimless crimes."

Franz brought the fish and then the wine and, although I would have poured the wine first, I let it slide. Mr. King did not appear to notice but I knew that he did.

*

I think we must have slept again for a while. I came awake suddenly, my head in her lap. Her fingers were moving lazily in my hair. I lifted my head and looked up and up through the valley of her breasts to that perfect face and that perfect smile.

"No one has ever done that to me before, Douglas. It was incredible. Thank you."

She rose slowly to a sitting position and cupped my face in her hands as I knelt before her in supplication.

"You have me all over your face," she said.

She bent to kiss me and I was impressed because I had been with women who wouldn't after you had and that made you wonder.

"Not half bad. I don't know what I was worried about."

She licked a long lick up my chin to the nose and then back to my lips for another kiss and then slipped backwards to resume her old position.

"Orgasms are quite exhausting," she said.

I moved up to join her. We lay for a while entwined with arms and legs until I rolled to her and said; "You're quite a dancer."

She laughed then, a real and hearty laugh that made her breasts roll and ripple and shimmy and if I have ever been in love with a woman, it was right then, with Sandy, with her beautiful breasts in my face and the music of her laughter and the smell of our sex all around and somewhere in the background I heard Paul, the DJ, saying that some song that I had missed had been for all the lovers out there. I could just picture Paul at the control panel with his grey mullet and bald on top with Joe, his much-younger husband. I saw me lying as I was with Sandy, the both of us freshly fucked and grandly so, and the whole situation struck me as more than a little unbelievable, ridiculous even. I laughed and laughed. I looked to her and said;

"Sandy, I need a drink. Can I get you one?"

She lifted her eyes for a brief moment and asked quite deadpan;

"Are you trying to get me drunk?"

We laughed to beat the band.

*

Mr. King and I declined dessert and he signed the bill. We lit postprandial cigarettes and smoked, making small talk amid the comfortable silence of digestion until he begged off to return to his duties.

"Miles to go and promises to keep and all that. Actually, a musical group and their entourage are checking in in a bit. He mentioned a name that everyone knew. They've taken the whole 5th Floor, God help us and save us. Have to make sure all the brown M and M's are removed."

He threw me a wink. I thought that anyone who buys me dinner and quotes Frost to me can't be half bad. As he left he gave me that look again, the one that made you feel like he's got you right by the soul.

"While I'm looking after my hotel, Mr. Edgars, is there anything I can do for you to make your stay more comfortable, more enjoyable?"

I decided to go for broke.

"I would kill for some weed, Mr. King. Marijuana. Pot. You know the story. My brain is so full right now. I just need to get away from myself and all these thoughts for a couple of days. I need to bleed off some pressure."

I wondered if he would think less of me for my weakness but he didn't blink an eye. He didn't miss a beat.

"I do not in any way condone the use of drugs, Mr. Edgars, but neither do I judge. Live and let live, sayeth the Lord."

He winked again and made the sign of the cross in my direction.

"I've heard rumours of some Hawaiian stuff circulating that I'm told is quite good. Charge it to your room?"

I nodded.

"I'll cancel maid service until further notice."

He winked again and left. I was left wondering if it had been worth it. I had developed a strong need to have this man like me. Franz came back and asked if everything had been satisfactory. I ordered a double stinger on the rocks and told him that Mr. King had said some nice things about him.

Franz beamed at me and I beamed right back at him. For the first time in some time I felt like I was hitting my stride. I felt like things just might turn out all right.

*

We drank our drinks and lay together. I had Sandy in a soft choke hold around the neck and we struggled up together.

"Will you promise me that if we get out of this bed, you won't put any clothes on," I asked?

I pulled her close for a kiss.

"But, Douglas...." She brushed my lips and pushed back against my chest until she was free.

"Where I come from, only bad girls and fallen women would parade around naked. My mother told me on the morning of my wedding that I should make sure to always come to bed covered up and in the dark and never let my husband see me in the altogether. That's what she called it, the altogether. I can just hear her. She was mortified to be having that conversation. She meant naked but couldn't say the word. She said that in the dark my husband would never know that my body was deteriorating. That was the extent of her pre-marriage advice. That and an uncomfortable trip to the doctor so he could explain things to me when I had my first period. I learned the rest from some girls at summer camp."

She gave me a wry smile. She was standing in front of me now. I pulled her to me and burrowed my face into her pubic hair. She was a brunette there too but hers was not a thick and wiry thatch. Her pubic hair was as dainty and soft as the rest of her and some curled into her as if they sought the same ultimate goal as I. The thought of that magnificent body deteriorating struck me as inordinately funny. I laughed out loud and struggled up beside her.

"I want you to be a fallen woman. That's the whole point. I want you to be a bad girl. As a matter of fact, I would like you to act the complete slut, Sandy. I can't speak for all men but what I want is a woman who can be demure in public and uninhibited, even a little wild, in private; one who isn't afraid to let her passions go, like you just did twice, or was it three times?"

She looked seriously at me to see if I was being serious. She smiled. "One slut coming up," she said.

She pulled me to my feet. With a vaudeville wiggle of her hips she pushed me past her and slapped my ass as I headed for the other room.

"I'll have another one of those sweet ones you made before," she said. "Maybe I'll have two. Then I really need a shower. I'm all sticky."

She ran past me and jumped onto the sofa like a naughty child and arranged herself until she became the most beautiful woman in the world sitting on a sofa. I mixed up another couple of Manhattans and took one to her. We sat and drank and kept our eyes closed silent, just me stroking her thigh and dallying in her pubic hair. On the radio, Paul introduced Cat Stevens' 'Tea for the Tillerman'. Things just kept getting better and better. I sat on the sofa with Sandy and listened to those beautiful melodies and smelled our sex and touched her and she touched me. Just when I thought I was losing my mind to the satisfaction and pleasure, she turned lazily up to me and whispered;

"Thank you, Douglas. This has been the best night of my life."

I rolled my head back to her. I was speechless. The best night of her life? This night had been my whole life. I pressed my fingers to my lips and then pushed them toward hers. She bit them first gently and then hard.

*

I had been back in my room no longer than twenty minutes when I heard a little knock and opened the door to a young bell-boy. He thrust a folded newspaper toward me.

"With Mr. King's compliments," he said.

Just another day at the office for him, within the bounds of human decency and the Nevada criminal code. I tipped him three hundred dollars.

Mr. King was true to his word. Wrapped in the paper was a two-ounce bag of big bud, resin-y pot, enough to keep me mellow for the next three days, give or take. A little pipe too, ivory I think, fancy anyway, and some wooden matches. I had been smoking weed since grade school. It had been my aunt's accidental discovery of my stash that had prompted her to send me to work. It had never been a social drug for me. When I was being social I snorted coke. Marijuana made me melt. Pot made conversation difficult; I seemed to always be two topics and twenty minutes behind the talk. Pot did allow me to recalibrate and sort though, to make sense of otherwise insensible things. I used pot as a holiday from other, more serious drugs. I had used it in school to help me read and study. I had used it when I wanted to appreciate the nuances of a movie. Now, I used it when I needed home for a rest.

I thought that I needed to think about Sandy and about the situation in which she had inexplicably placed me. I needed it to help shuffle some mental cards. I needed it to get the lay of the land. I certainly couldn't do it clean and sober. I didn't want to even try to do it clean and sober. I was tight. I was a clockwork. I was a spring. I needed to let myself slowly and safely unwind. I knew I couldn't do it drunk, too sloppy, too much danger of losing control. I needed something else. I took to that Hawaiian like a duck to water.

*

Eventually our finger biting led to kissing and the kissing led to caresses and the caresses led us back to bed. I was slow to get hard.

"Use your mouth, Sandy," I asked. She did and she did. When I was diamond cutting hard, harder than I'd ever been, she smiled up from my erection to me and gave me another helping of that little girl bicycle grin; "I did it." She held me firmly in her fist like a gear shift.

"You sure did. You did it beautifully. Although, you know, they say a woman is not really good at that particular skill until she's done it ten thousand times."

"Nine thousand nine hundred ninety-nine to go," she said.

I rolled on top and slid inside. I paused there for a long moment just enjoying the fit of her.

"I want to finish it some time. I want to drink you," she said.

"I want that too," I said.

We made sweet love this time. We had the sex of the angels, slow and sweet with music. We made the beast with two backs, her arms and her legs tight around me. We made sweet love this time. We had the sex of the angels, slow and sweet with music. We slept in a tangle of arms, a complication of legs.

*

Mr. King was true to his word. The Hawaiian was just what the doctor ordered. The Hawaiian did me a world of good. Almost immediately, I came to appreciate the luxurious freedom of being totally fucked up but safe and rich as hell in a first-class hotel in a city that never sleeps. There was an apparently infinite stream of bell boys at the other end of the telephone to cater to all my whims. There was room service. I upgraded my television to a very big, big-screen and added a DVD player. I acquired a nice laptop and shopped for movies online. I bought all the movies I remembered loving but had never watched. I bought movies that I had never heard of. Episode after episode, season after season of my favourite old sit-coms. I bought a stereo and all the music I could think of. I ordered books I never read. I ordered intermittent meals at all hours. I smoked and drank the mini-bar dry. Like magic it was refilled again and again. I tipped everyone who came near me a crisp hundred-dollar bill.

I emptied my mind. I lost track of night and day. I lost track of the passage of time. I would smoke and smoke until I could smoke no more. I would drink something when I felt dry. I would stare at some screen or some printed world and listen to some sounds and pretend to be considering my options. I slept here and there, now and then. Mostly, I sat on my balcony and stared at the lights and the sights of the city.

I allowed my mind to wander. Sometimes I was with Sandy. Sometimes I was with old restaurant friends. Mostly I was alone. Sometimes I relived past lives. Sometimes I strayed back to the horror that was Mary and scurried home to smoke some more in self-defence. Sometimes there was my Aunt Marie, snoring gently in an armchair. Sometimes my Mom and Dad sat with me; Mom, who I knew mostly by sense of touch, the memory of a smell and the perhaps recollection of a certain pleasant feeling; Dad, who I knew hardly at all. I don't think my Dad had been around much. When I pictured his face, I saw it through the front window of our house. I saw him behind the wheel of the car. He is driving away. My most vivid memory of my father was his voice. That voice, that voice memory, will not leave me. My Mother smiling, watching us from the house. I remember my Dad pushing me on my first two-wheeler and yelling at me when I fell. It was red, that first two-wheeler. It gleamed in the sun and I was very proud. It was the best bike in the neighbourhood. I remember crying. I had ripped the knee of my pants on the sidewalk when I fell. There was some little bit of blood. I remember my Dad's voice when my Mom came out to see.

"He's not even trying," my dad had said and he walked into the house.

My Mother gathered me up and took me inside for a cold drink and a bandage. I had been trying my very hardest to learn to ride that bike. When a boy saw his dad as seldom as I did, he tried his very hardest every time. My Dad was gone and I learned to ride that bike by myself the next day by rolling slowly down the driveway again and again until I discovered the miracle of balance. I yelled for my mother to come out to watch. She raised her hands to her mouth as if to scream as I rolled toward the busy street but her fear turned to laughter and squeals and hand clapping as I safely negotiated the turn down the sidewalk and ped-alled safely back. That night at dinner she served me a fresh-baked cookie with a candle in to celebrate my prowess. It had been just the two of us. Before my next birthday and before my next candle, she and my father would both be dead. I would be living with my Aunt Marie. There was no room in her little apartment for a bike. There was no safe place nearby to ride it. She lived downtown and the traffic was incessant.

*

Sandy and I woke together in the earliest dawn of the morning and made love again. We were a practised, polished team now, Sandy molding herself to me and thrusting as I pushed, Sandy pulling me in as I pulled away. She had starting doing things with her hands that left me panting. When we were done she glanced to the bedside clock.

"Douglas, I'm supposed to meet my friends in an hour. What am I going to do with you?"

I, ever the joker, said;

"Let's run away together."

She fixed me with another of those too long looks.

"Let me think about that."

By the time she was out of the shower she had it all worked out.

"Okay. Here's what we can do. I'll do brunch and a last matinee with my friends," she said. "After that we were all going to the airport and leaving for home. I can make something up. I can say I'm going to visit an old friend who lives in the city. I'll say she's going through a bad divorce, which is true, and she wants some comforting. We could hole up in the city for a few days and spend some more time together."

She was excited now. She was talking fast.

"Would you like that? I guess I should have asked you about it first. I've never done anything like this before and I'm pretty sure I've gone insane."

She became slow and cautious and careful. She was looking up at me. Her eyes were stars. She had her hands soft on my shoulders.

"I mean, you're not sick of me already are you? My husband is in New York on business for another two weeks. I'll tell him that some of us girls decided to do a little shopping. He'll never miss me."

I, who had missed her like I was short of breath while she was in the shower, was aghast at an attitude so cavalier with such precious a gift. I was thinking ten things at once. My head was a pinball machine. I said nothing. I stood, mouth open, looking down at her like I was feeble-minded.

"Do you think you can get away," she asked?

She looked at me like she was looking at a person who might not be able to get away and I, who could gather my entire life into a steamer trunk at the drop of a hat, said sure. I phoned work and lied to the boss about some unfinished business in the city and got the time off, easy enough so early in the season. While Sandy brunched and matinee-ed, I went back to my room and gathered all the things I thought I'd need and met her back at The Belmont. The step-sisters had gone on without her and hadn't batted an eye at the change of plans. The step-sisters were, Sandy said, so self-absorbed that they had barely paid attention. The step-sisters had air-kissed and chattered and left. The step-sisters were apparently, none the wiser. Sandy was out of sight, out of mind. None of them, I supposed, could ever imagine Sandy the sweet being so duplicitous.

I was becoming more and more sure that I had become insane. I had done some crazy, off-the-cuff things in my time but this one appeared to be a personal best. I reluctantly brought up the subject of money. I had been able to put together three hundred dollars in cash, which was most of my next rent payment. Without work where was that going to come from? It's not like I had something put aside for a rainy day. I told her so. She smiled. Her eyes were supernovas now.

"Not to worry, sweet heart."

She had taken to calling me 'sweetheart' and I, who had once kissed a woman off for suggesting that I give her a key to my place, was in love with the possessive sound of the word from her lips. She was playful. She was kind. She was determined. Not for the first time, I felt decidedly out of my league.

"You leave all that to me. I am quite a wealthy woman, you know, in addition to being beautiful and intelligent and a fantastic lover. I have a magic card that will take us anywhere we want to go. I can buy us a small country of our own if we'd like, a warm tropical one with banana plantations and smiling natives with fans and, if that doesn't work, I have some other things that are just as good, better in some circum- stances. I am not, Sir, without feminine wiles."

That ended all the money talk. She flashed her American Express card at the hotel front desk clerk. She flashed her American Express card at the driver of the limo with the smoked glass divider between pas- sengers and driver. We were soon settled in for the 2- hour ride to the city. She had ordered the limo stocked with champagne and cheese and bread and olives. We ate and drank and talked and laughed. Somewhere down the highway, I threw her bra out the sun roof into the wind and made her promise to go without one for a week. She had agreed. We had necked and dry- humped and we had giggled like teenagers when we knew the parents wouldn't be home for hours and hours and hours.

I was six years old when my parents were killed and I went to live with my father's sister, Marie. She was my only relative on either side. I had never met her. She and my father had not been close.

Aunt Marie was a waitress in a diner at the edge of a big town on a big highway catering to tourists and truckers mostly. She worked hard from ten 'til two and five 'til eight, five days a week, Mondays and Tuesdays off, minimum wage plus tips, ten per cent on a good day. When she came home in the afternoon she had a drink or two or three and napped in her easy chair. When she came home at night, she had a drink or two or three and fell asleep in front of the television with her feet – her 'dogs' she called them – in a bucket of hot water. Aunt Marie had no children of her own. She had been briefly married once. Her ex-husband, she told me and everyone who would listen, a deadbeat and a tomcat and a bastard.

I was often left alone in her little apartment above the music store with the door locked and the television for company and TV dinners to sustain me and promises to be a good boy and go to bed at the assigned time. There was no money for babysitters. There was no money for lots of things.

I was a child of my century. I watched 'Rowan and Martin's Laugh-In'. Seeing Goldie Hawn in a gold lamé bikini brought my first sexual yearnings.

I watched the war in Vietnam every night on the news. I learned to recognize the different types of helicopter gunships and cheer the body-count numbers that showed definitively that the good guys were winning. I ate dinner most nights with Walter Cronkite and imagined that he was my father. I imagined that a lot of men were my father. I watched transfixed as Bobby Kennedy was shot in some hotel kitchen. I bled with Reverend King on a hotel balcony in some squalid southern town. I liked the Saturday cartoons but I got up early on Sunday mornings too to watch the news and the political talk shows. I became a conservative because the righteousness I saw on television made it right. I stayed up very late to watch the moon landing. I watched Nixon and his troubles. I became a cynic.

I grew up alone. Aunt Marie worked from ten 'til two and five 'til eight, five days a week, Mondays and Tuesdays off, for minimum wage plus tips, ten per cent on a good day and drank her drinks and soaked her dogs and did her best. When I reached a certain age, I was allowed the freedom of the neighbourhood. When she started to worry about me getting involved with girls and booze and drugs and petty crime, she brought me to work with her. I started in the dish pit. My illustrious career was born. Half my wages went back to Aunt Marie. Half I kept. I was a pay day millionaire. I was a pauper.

I graduated from dishwasher to prep cook to short-order cook. When I learned just how much more money the waitstaff made and how little they worked for it, I moved to the dining room as a busboy and from there to better restaurant downtown. I was the hors d'oeuvre guy who pushed a little cart around to tables that had just ordered dinner and offered them nibbles of asiago cheese and artichoke hearts and pickled vegetables and salami and provolone and fancy crackers to munch while they waited for their dinners of steak and lobster and coq au vin. Half my wages went back to Aunt Marie. I kept all my tips to myself. I was a pauper.

It was in that better restaurant downtown that I lost my technical virginity to Alice, a loud, busty and lusty French-Canadian waitress. Catching me eavesdropping on a conversation she was having with a couple of the other waitresses about her latest boyfriend and his remarkable virility, she told me simply; "Come here." I was 14.

She gave me my first kiss, my first caress of a warm, soft, full breast, and my first blowjob inside the walk-in fridge where I stocked my cart before service – me with quaking knees, pants around my ankles, my naked ass pressed against freezing stainless-steel shelving, Alice kneeling in front of me, kneeling on a soiled tablecloth lest the concrete damage her hose – and changed my life. I went from being a boy without a clue to a boy who knew the exquisite pleasure of an expertly administered blowjob. I was never sure when I became a man.

I became a waiter at that restaurant part-time during school and full-time on holidays and during the summer. When high school was done and my scholarship to a city university was not enough to cover my bills, I returned part-time to the restaurant business. I never really left. Aunt Marie's noble plan to keep me pure of heart through good honest labour and the moral lessons inherent in earning my keep was a non-starter. Instead, I discovered drugs and booze and girls and the easy life early in the neighbourhood. I perfected drugs and booze and girls and the easy life in the restaurant business. I acquired an expensive life style. I became as phony as the job required. I became full of shit.

*

Sandy and I checked in to the Princess, an exquisite, little boutique hotel on the expensive edge of the city's downtown in the early evening. We didn't leave our suite for two days. Our life was room service meals and mini-bar drinks and hiding, giggling like fools, on the balcony while the maid changed the sheets and restocked the towels and the F and B people brought us more mini-bottles and took away the dead soldiers.

In spite of her inexperience (maybe because of her inexperience) Sandy took to sex in a big way. Sandy was a natural. Sandy was a prodigy. Sandy was precocious. She wanted to do it, do it all and do it everywhere in every way. I was in hog heaven. She wanted to talk about it and discuss it and study it like a schoolgirl. I became the willing tutor. I was hands on. We studied each others' privates like a treasure map and got to know them as never before. She masturbated me and squealed with glee as I fountained back onto my chest. She licked me clean. She spread wide for me like a gynaecological exam. I examined her body like a new toy for it was that for us both. I shaved her. I introduced her to the soft-core porn of the hotel's adult television pay-per-view. I taught her dirty words she had never dreamed of. She taught me to stroke a woman's hair and talk nonsense baby-talk into her ear until she fell asleep. When we woke we started it again. It never paled.

*

My first real and extended sex and love affair happened during high school. My partner was a little older than I, vastly more experienced and worldly, wise, eager to show her young charge the niceties and nasties of sexual life. Her parents went away to their cottage every weekend in the summer, leaving us free to indulge ourselves in comfort and safety in the comfort of her parents' split-level home. While my classmates and their partners struggled and contorted themselves in the backseats of their parents' cars or hid shivering in the bushes at the edge of town, we fucked in the lap of luxury. Everything I had read, everything I had seen in the grainy pornographic films that circulated before the world wide web turned porn into commonplace, everything I imagined and everything I thought I invented was available to me. I revelled in the lessons. I yearned for them. I was ungrateful. When I had taken all that I thought I could take, learned all the teacher had to teach me, I spurned that teacher for a finer, fresher student of my own. Where is she now, my voracious darling, my red-haired girl, my tutor? I wonder. Where is she now, my apprentice, my hungry student?

I found her again with Sandy. I answered all her questions and showed her all I knew. I was gentle and tireless and kind. I taught her to masturbate. I fell asleep and woke in her mouth. I wiped her clean when she pissed. She gave her all. I could not get enough. I would never get enough.

*

On the third day in my Hawaiian-infused heaven, I remembered the note Sandy had written to me and decided that the time had come to read it. I reproduce it here in full.

Darling Douglas,

(I stopped here for weeping as I saw her spidery, feminine script for the first time; how I had loved her hands and how her hands had loved me. How I had loved that she was so little.)

> *Kisses to you my sweet, sweet heart. I hope this message finds you an old and happy man, for if you are reading this letter it means that I am dead and I have no wish for that. I have just begun to live. If that is the case, I give you all of these things in an attempt to pay you back for all that you gave me. We had only one week I know, but that week was my whole life in so many ways and another life besides and another life after that, one that is just between you and I. Things will never convey my thanks, my appreciation, my love but things are all I have. Not a waking hour has passed that I have not thought of you. I smile often for no apparent reason. My friends think I am*

insane. I am a better person now. I am a better wife. I can never repay you for all of that and what came after but I can try. Take all of this and enjoy your life. Be with other women. Give them life like you gave me. Right some wrongs. Spread our laughter. Spread the sweetness we shared. I loved you although we never talked much of that. I love you now. I loved your loving me. I feel it still. It is the very nicest feeling.
Sandy

She had finished with a row of scrawled Xs and Os. I lost it.

*

Love. We had mentioned the word just once that I could recall. It was on our second last day together, perhaps the third, the Saturday, perhaps the Friday night. We had finished making love for the millionth time – we were so very good at it now – and had rolled into our accustomed after-action positions, me on my back, right arm behind her neck pulling her to me slightly. Her on her left side, head on my shoulder, right arm toying across my chest, right leg thrown across mine. I remember feeling her drip on to my thigh. I wouldn't have moved for the world. It was early evening. It was rush hour. The noise of traffic outside was considerable through the open balcony door. From somewhere there was music, maybe the TV.

"Do you suppose you love me, Douglas," she whispered?

(She had a curious way of using the word 'suppose' instead of 'think' or 'wonder' or 'imagine' that made me wonder if I had ever used any of those words correctly.)

"Yes," I replied. "I suppose I do. I must. There's no other way to explain it."

I was drowsy, sated. My eyes were mostly closed.

"Explain what," she asked?

"All of this," I replied. "You know. Everything we've done. The way you make my heart feel."

"Oh that," she said after a while and curled herself more tightly to me.

"I love you back, I suppose," she said. "I love you this instant, this right here, this way, like this, you and I. I love the way you make my heart feel."

She said this with some finality. We fell asleep. We spoke no more of it. We didn't need to. We lived it for another day or two. Love is amorphous like that. Love is like water is to the fish. You never notice it when you're swimming in it every day. You don't feel it when it's in your hair and in your eyes and in your lungs. You don't recognize it when you're dizzy from its perfume, pungent, dangerous, edgy like gasoline, as satisfying as your favourite childhood food, sweet like honey. More's the pity. La Rochefoucauld, he of the maxims, wrote;

"The pleasure of love is in loving and there is more joy in the passion one feels than in that which one inspires."

Were La Rochefoucauld here right now I would

laugh in his silly French face and call him a fraud and a poser and a *dilettante*. I'm thinking La Rochefoucauld never felt love like I felt love with Sandy. I'm thinking La Rochefoucauld never saw someone smile a Sandy smile, never saw the sex flush spread like a ribbon across her chest, never heard her sigh or gasp or whisper sweet, never saw a rivulet of sweat work its way from her hairline to her forehead, across a delicate cheek and chin, never saw that drop pick up speed as gravity grabbed it somewhere between her perfect breasts, never saw that drop splash in a slow sort of motion near my navel, where it burned like some pleasant, addictive acid. La Rochefoucauld never felt the grip of her thighs, the strength in her arms, the very heat of her. La Rochefoucauld never heard the timbre of her voice as she thanked me for something that was so beautiful it broke your heart every time. I'm thinking La Rochefoucauld didn't know shit from Shinola really. I'm thinking La Rochefoucauld never kissed a girl. He certainly never kissed my Sandy.

*

When I had smoked the last pipe, I slept for a long while. I took a long shower, dressed in some of my new duds and got on the phone to Mr. King to invite myself to dinner at ten. He agreed most graciously.

"Decided to rejoin the living, did you? he asked."

I allowed that I had.

"One other thing, Mr. Edgars. You leave that pot in your room, will you. I don't judge but I prefer to talk to the real man."

I told him that the real man, such as he was, had finally found his way back to the present and was hungry for the living and the dinner.

*

On our third day together in the city, Sandy and I ventured out to dinner. I knew a bunch of great places and had even worked in some but I told her that we would never be able to find a table at an hour's notice even if I begged and pleaded and called in all of my markers. You simply could not pull a rabbit out of an empty hat, I told her. I hated myself and I hated the world for disappointing her. Sandy just smiled and asked me the name of the best place in town. I told her and she told me to get dressed and she called downstairs for a car. As we left she filled my hand with a fat wad of hundred-dollar bills and said that when her magic card didn't work the magic of cold hard cash always did.

"I'm sure you know how to work with these, Douglas," she said.

I did. Three of the hundreds into the pocket of the tuxedo at the door got us in and two more got us a table in a cozy corner and the wine list. After that, things went very smoothly indeed. We pulled the rabbit out of the hat after all.

When we walked out of the restaurant after the best dinner I ever had, Sandy took my hands in hers and pressed her panties into them. They were a whisper of a thing, warm and damp.

"I took them off in the ladies' room the last time."

Her eyes were twinkling with mischief.

"I suppose now that you know I'm defenceless under this little slip of a dress, you want to take me home
and ravage me, you beast of a man?"

She was pressing her chest into my arm and her
pelvis into my hip in an alarming fashion and pulling
me toward the street.

"Actually," I said, "I thought we'd go dancing. I
know how much you love dancing and I know a great
little place for music."

I smiled my own mischief. She gave a little mewl in
protest. I steered her out the door by the elbow and
asked the doorman to hail us a cab.

The magic hundreds worked again to get us into the
little penthouse piano bar at the top of the Plaza Hotel
and got us a nice table too. Knowing that Sandy was
without her underwear (I had tossed them to the restaurant doorman to see her blush as we got into the
cab) had us both a little on edge. We got to our table
just as the band was starting a set so we danced before we drank, cheek to chest and hip to thigh. When
the band rested so did we. I ordered us a bottle of
Bollinger, the good stuff, '68, no fucking around with
domestic, and watched the waiter jump to the bar and
laughed as the barman jumped to the fridges and
watched them all jump for the wine bucket and the
$600 a bottle ceremony and fixings. Sandy and I
toasted and drank and watched the lights of the city
out the window. We toyed with each other under the
table cloth. We discussed the best bits of what we had
done and what we thought we might like to do again

and do next. When the bottle was upside down in its bucket and the musicians had taken their final bows we stood to leave. She pulled me to her, and said;

"Douglas, you'd better walk close behind me. I'm sure there's a big wet spot on the back of my skirt."

I laughed – I had never laughed the way I laughed during those days with Sandy – and gathered her before me in the folds of my jacket. With her little fist tightly curled around the shaft of my erection like a blind woman clutching her cane, she led me to the elevator and into the cab and back to our nest.

*

Mr. King gave me the once over a couple of times as I sat. I knew he was looking for signs of the drugs on me. Fair enough. I gave him my eyes and let him look to his heart's content. When he was satisfied and we had made small talk and passed the time of day, I showed Mr. King the letter from Sandy. I had told him some of the story. I felt that it would have been unfair to him to withhold the maybe ending. He put on little half-glasses and read it carefully twice. Finished, he carefully refolded it into the envelope and slid it across the table to me. He was silent for long enough for me to start to become uncomfortable.

"So, what are you going to do, Mr. Edgars?"

I let out a long breath. I grinned.

"I'm going to spread some sweetness and right some wrongs, Mr. King. Somebody better warn Riley because as of now I start living his life."

We talked of many things that night, he and I,

mostly about my life before and during Sandy and a little about my life after and a little about my life to come. Mr. King was as fine a listener as he was a teller of tales. We had a nice dinner, served by Franz again – two salads of tomato and bocconcini, two rare peppercorn steaks prepared table side, *creme caramel* for dessert. I had a glass of some obscure Oregon white with the salad and a half-bottle of heavy Napa Valley red with the steak. Mr. King stuck with sparkling water. Franz was on his game that night. After dessert it was Remy for me and black coffee for him. I asked him if he knew any women. He smiled and assured me that he did. I asked him if he'd introduce me to some women. He smiled. Mr. King let me pay. I made Franz's week.

*

When I finished my undergraduate degree, I didn't look for a career job. I was lazy and disinterested and uncertain. To pay the bills, I went back to the lucrative comfort and ease of the restaurant business. I had no intention of going any further in school and looked upon my colleagues taking entry-level junior office clerk jobs with the government or some bank or insurance company with horror and pity. I went back to the lucrative comfort and ease of the restaurant business. I did well. I was soon working as the *maître d'* of a prestigious little city club in the centre of the downtown financial district; no sports, just a couple of nice dining rooms, some guest bedroom suites and meeting rooms, and a dark and woody basement bar for those barons of industry who didn't want to appear in public with dates who may not have been their wives.

Life was sweet. The club worked bankers' hours and so did I. It was open four days a week, closed Friday and the weekend. Like Aunt Marie, I worked the split shift, ten 'til two and five 'til ten. I was making a boatload of money, most of it backhanded and tax free. I had a satisfying and purely physical thing going with a high school aged bus girl who had proved to be as sexually curious and insatiable as she was demure. I should have been in hog heaven. I was unhappy, listless, incomplete. At home in my tiny apartment, I read and reread the classics. I poured my thoughts into a journal. I wrote bad, derivative poetry. I took too many of all kinds of drugs. I drank all the time. After about 6 months, I met an erstwhile professor of mine on the street. He had taught me much about history and seemed to like me. I liked him. I had taken every course he offered. We had gotten to know each other a bit although we had not become friends. That meeting on the street led to a boozy lunch at the end of which he took me to task for what he considered my waste of a life.

"Douglas, you're a natural scholar. You read history and it lives for you. You write history better than most, if not all, of the people who taught your courses, present company excepted, of course. It pains me to hear of you wasting your talents slopping the hogs of the bourgeoisie. Let me make a call."

What he said hit home but I demurred until one

night I got into it with a thieving bartender and a belligerent drunken patron and completed the trifecta with a nasty jealous scene with the high school aged bus girl. I finished the night alone with a bottle of port. The next morning, I called the good professor and told him I had had enough. He was right. I asked him if he would make his calls. He was as good as his word. I was soon enrolled as a graduate student in the faculty of history at a decent little college in a decent little city with a decent little annual stipend. My rootless, shiftless restaurant days were over, exchanged for the richer, rarified atmosphere of academe. I almost bought a tweed jacket with leather patches at the elbows. I seriously considered smoking a pipe.

On my first day as a graduate student in the faculty of history at a decent little college in a decent little city with a decent little annual stipend, I was welcomed and oriented and given a long list of my duties and responsibilities. The first of these was that I was expected to lead a group of first year students in a discussion of the Treaty of Versailles the next day. I was keen. I took the course prospectus and the text book to a little conference room to arrange my thoughts. Versailles was an interesting enough treaty and one that I knew well but I had never had to tell others just what it was I thought I knew. As I sat there thinking and planning and arranging and gathering wool, she bounced in. She was wearing a little Cindi Lauper skirt and jacket. She tossed herself onto the conference table in front of me and said;

"So. You're the new guy?"

I looked up past her boots, past her skinny thighs, past the little flash of white panty between her legs to her wild mane of red hair and said;

"Yes. I suppose I am. Who are you?"

I was a little pissy. I was really planning to give this school thing an honest go. I resented her loud and rude interruption. I resented her familiarity.

"I'm Mary," she said. "I've got the other half of that class."

She dismissed the work in front of me with a sniff and a toss of her chin.

"Listen. Why don't you buy me a coffee and I'll tell you who's zoomin' who around here."

I did. She did. That's how I met Mary. That's how my right went all wrong.

*

I had asked Mr. King to introduce me to a tall, leggy blonde. He was as good as his word. I had been in my room just long enough for a shower and a beer and a half before the knock on the door.

"Mr. Edgars. I'm Nancy. Mr. King sent me."

I smiled as best I could, suddenly nervous, and ushered her in. She was tall and leggy and very beautiful and very blonde. I thought I would never have another petite brunette in my life. Nancy and I sat and drank and chatted for much of the night. I thought it went well enough, my first experience with a prostitute, except for the not having sex part and the crying part. We sat and drank and chatted for most of the night. We laughed a few laughs. We listened to some music and somewhere among the drinks and the music and the conversation, we decided that sex under the present circumstances might be counter-productive. For me. I told her my story. I had become a regular magpie, spilling my guts to everyone I met. Nancy cried at the best bits and when she left she gave me a nice hug and a sweet and chaste kiss goodbye. We agreed that we would meet again but we both knew better. I was in no position for another woman. I was in no position at all. I went to bed alone that night, happy except for the crying. I had become a regular Pollyanna in the tears department. I snivelled at the drop of a hat. There would be no escorts for me. I wondered if there would be sex. Masturbation had become a sad and terrible labour.

*

Sandy and I spent seven days and nights together before she left for her home and me for mine. I figured I had thirty orgasms in or on or around her. Sandy had the same, probably more. Sometimes I wasn't sure if she had two in a row or just one long, pounding one. I worked hard to please her. I concentrated. I did not shirk. I worked until she would push me away.

Once while we were getting ready for a dinner out, I took her from behind while she was leaning into the bathroom mirror fixing her face. She had been naked and working hard with a little brush at something to do with eyes. She had been ready. She had been willing. I had been brief.

"Every time I see you, it's like I have to be inside you."

"That's okay, Douglas," she breathed. "That's what I want too. I want it so much and I want it again and again."

She reached between her thighs to tickle my balls. I was spent, shrinking.

"Every time you see me, Douglas, every time. Take what you want. I'll never say no. Never. I don't think I can."

And sometimes it was...

"Time for my lesson," she would say, and bend to her task.

"Are you watching me?" she would ask, suddenly shy about halfway through.

"I can't take my eyes off you," I would reply in all honesty.

She would look from my cock to my face to my cock to my face and she would blush and smile. When we were done she would kiss me shyly and ask;

"Was that okay?"

I would smile. I would say that was the best ever. She would smile. She would say, nine thousand, nine hundred and however many to go.

And sometimes...

I would tell her of the Muslim martyrs of the Koran who had been promised a paradise where orgasms would last for a thousand years. She would laugh and say she much preferred lots of the old-fashioned kind and we would go to work.

And sometimes...

I would smile until I thought my face would break.

And sometimes...

She would trace the lines on my face with her lips and her nose and her eyelashes and her tongue.

We were always late for dinner.

*

I settled in. I became a fixture at Mr. King's grand hotel. I got comfortable. I was out of control. I became part of the family. I hid. I isolated. I gambled in the casino and I ate in the dining room and I drank in the bars. I got to know the staff by first name. They got to know me because I tipped everyone who came near me with a hundred-dollar bill. I dodged the lawyers. I stayed pretty much drunk all the time. I would have gone on like that forever. Mr. King was the adult in the room.

"It's time for you to go, Mr. Edgars. You know it is. You're spinning your wheels here. You're just killing time and I think you might be killing yourself. It's time to get yourself straightened around. Time to face the music."

I saw myself through his eyes. I saw the old Douglas, flying by the seat of his pants, hiding behind the noise and the lights of the party, avoiding the toils of life, avoiding responsibility, avoiding consequences. I saw the old Douglas, afraid to consider the past, afraid to face what I had become, not knowing what would become of me. In my heart of hearts where all things try to hide, I was scared to death. In my heart of hearts where all things try to hide, I was paralyzed. In my heart of hearts where all things try to hide, I knew Sandy would not approve. In my heart of hearts, I knew that Sandy had made me something else; something before she died and yet another thing after. Something better. I knew it when I was sober. I could drink it away for a while but I always knew it when I was sober. Sandy would be ashamed of me.

I had no argument for Mr. King. I went to my room, pissed as a newt, fished a business card from the back of my wallet and placed the call to Reid/Carruthers in San Francisco. It was the middle of the night. I reached some disinterested answering service operator who assured me she would pass the message along. I left my number. In the time it took for me to have a piss and shake it dry, the phone was ringing. I answered it to a panic-stricken Reid or an overcome Carruthers. I had never learned to tell them apart. Whoever was on the telephone implored me to come to San Francisco right away. Immediately. Right then. He pleaded as if his life depended on it. I wondered if it did. I was not familiar with the ways of lawyers. There were papers to sign, he said, and worlds to save and I don't know what all else. My, how he went on, convincing me in an endless stream of lawyer words of something that Mr. King had convinced me of with a word. I asked him to book me a suite in the Biltmore. Mr. King had told me it was the only really first-class hotel in San Francisco and I knew he would never steer me wrong. There was no problem with that. I asked him to arrange for a private plane. There was no problem with that. I got the impression I could have asked for the moon on a plate with a side of stars and he wouldn't have flinched. I assured him I would be there in the morning. I hung up the phone. I packed my new clothes in my new luggage. I took once last look around the rooms that had been my home for so long. I called Chester to get me to the airport. As I reached the revolving door to the hotel, I caught Mr. King's eye or perhaps he caught mine. He was just at the door to his little office off the main lobby. His telephone was pressed to his ear. He didn't appear interested in what he was hearing. I thought he might have been on hold. He gave me a nod and a wink. He raised a silent hand. I left with tears in my eyes. Despite a life lived alone, I had never felt more alone. I was afraid too, scared to death. I remembered one of Aunt Marie's favourite sayings. She pulled it out ever time I faced a challenge.

"You only have to be brave for 20 seconds, Douglas. Anybody can be brave for 20 seconds."

I thought I would have to be brave for a lot longer than 20 seconds this time. I thought I would have to be brave considerably longer than that. I thought I might have to be brave for the rest of my life. I would have to be brave because it was for Sandy. Down deep, I didn't think I had it in me.

*

Now comes the time, dear reader, when the writer becomes uncomfortable with his tale, the time when the primal urge is to pull back into the shell. That, despite the things, the most personal things, I have said to date. It is always easier to write of the good than the bad, the future and the past than the present. The past is *trompe-l'oeil* faded. The present is ugly and unabashed. To write about Mary would be like writing about the present for me. Mary had owned my heart and treated it rough. For all my bravado, I thought she might own it still. For that I was 10 times a fool and 10 times a cuckold and 10 times worse besides, weaker, more stupid, pitiful. Despite all the beauty I had shared with Sandy, I had ugly to spare. It was always just there, just beneath the surface, scar tissue now but still painful. I still felt roaring phantom pains from long ago hurts, wounds, amputations.

There was a period in my life just after university when I read nothing but autobiographical tales of soldiers. Which war didn't matter. I was just interested in the lyrical transformation from citizen to soldier to hero and back again to citizen. I can't remember why this was for the life of me. I went through phases.

I read one such tale of an American WW II flier downed in Burma or some other godforsaken jungle shit-hole. He lost his arm in the crash. Hanging from a tree by the shreds of his parachute, he had to cut himself clear, cut himself clear at the elbow to fall to the jungle floor. He wandered the jungle, delirious, starving, hurting, sick. He stewed in fear and anger and self-pity. He becomes convinced in his malarial fever thoughts that there are maggots growing under the bandage he has rigged to cover his half arm. Knowing full well he is crazy, raving, mistaken, he peels off the bandage and rips off the scab only to find all things underneath pink and healthy. I feel like that flyer now as I toy with this scab, one I have carried for too long. I am convinced that there are things under there that are poison. I am convinced that maggots dine there. They feast on me. I can smell the rot of the flesh.

On the short flight to San Francisco in the private plane, I slept. While I slept, I dreamed of witches. They chased me on brooms.

*

I suppose the fact that Mary was married when she fucked me that first day should have been the giveaway. From coffee we had progressed to drinks at the graduate student pub and then to my new, barely slept-in bed. I arrived at my discussion group the next morning dehydrated and much the worse for wear. I was ill-prepared but still, I thought, coherent. Thus, it began. It stayed the same. It got worse.

Mary filled my life as never before. I allowed it. I welcomed it. I could not stop. From a trivial and pacific life of mindless work and brainless girlfriend, I came to live inside the maelstrom. Mary challenged me for the first time as an intellectual equal or more than equal. My understated, confident, pinstripe, *New Republic* liberalism was no match for her strident, indignant, 'to the barricades' *The Nation* Marxism. Physically too, she dominated me. My appetites were a mere pang next to her consuming hungers. She would disappear for a day or two or three and return without a word of explanation, without missing a beat. She gave away nothing. She took at will. My own life, such as it had become, was on hold the entire time. I held my breath. I was in heaven. I was in hell. The angel in her would sometimes torture my soul. The devil in her would thrill me with kisses. She used sex sometimes as a weapon and sometimes as a prize. She used sex sometimes as a bludgeon and sometimes as a feather. She surprised even jaded me with the carnal depths to which we sank. Buried in her ass, ("I don't like it physically," she said. "I like it psychologically. It's so deliciously dirty to have a cock in me where I shit."), she would hector me about the United Mine Workers and their wobbly, watery support of Theodore Roosevelt in 1900. With my cock in her slash of a mouth, she would drive me to admit that Wilson had given away the farm in 1919 to the detriment of a lasting peace and international socialism. I readily agreed to any and all. I would have agreed to anything. I was lost. She begged me to piss in her face in the tub and then left me to sleep on the couch, the bedroom door slammed and locked in my face. Perhaps because I had pissed too much, perhaps too little, perhaps because I had dared to piss at all. One never knew for sure, not with Mary. Mary changed. Mary was the weather. Mary was aggressor and victim both. She told me terrible tales of her drunken mother and her shadow father. She showed me vicious red scars of self-mutilation. I gathered her to me and kissed up her tears. She came at me with a steak knife once and I raped her in self-defence on the kitchen floor. We laughed it off. We laughed everything off. There was often screaming. Life with Mary was never quiet. Mary changed. Mary was the weather.

A couple of months into that first term we were living together and her divorce was in the works. I suspected she was still fucking her husband. She did nothing to allay my fears. She encouraged them. She laughed at them. She continued to teach me and challenge me and torture me. I continued as the lickspittle I had become. I was oblivious. I was blind. I was stupid. I was dumb.

One is never aware of the depth of their sinking. Putrid sewage water all round me, I saw only blue lagoon. Fresh air I breathed deep, unaware that I was ten feet under. Mary was no high-school bus girl. Mary was no Alice, the waitress in the walk-in fridge. Mary was my *houri*. Mary ruled me like some wicked, insane despot. I loved her for deigning to rule me at all.

At the end of our year Mary accepted a position at a good school on the coast to do her doctorate; she was a half-year ahead of me in academic terms. I was to follow her there after the next term. The plan was that I would complete my thesis and enter the PhD program there behind her. PhDs in hand, we would change the world, she and I. We had it all figured out.

Mary left for the coast in January. I joined her in July. Nothing changed. We were in and out of touch. We were in and out of synch. We were in and out of love. We fucked mostly angry now. We lived angry. We continued this frenetic, schizophrenic existence until

December. I returned East to attend the Christmas wedding of a friend. Mary and I made our tearful good-byes. When the wedding festivities and the holiday were over and I was about to come home, I called.

"I've decided it's not working between us, Douglas," she said. "What we have is just not healthy. I've given this a lot of thought. I don't want you to come back. I'll send your stuff."

I could not argue with the argument's essentials. Along with my irrational love, I had acquired irrational jealousy and developed stupid suspicions, both exacerbated by insanity and ego and drug use and constant drinking, hers and mine. Yet, still I argued, confident that intellectual discussion would bring this problem to a more positive resolution. I argued and I pleaded until she brought the argument to an abrupt end by proclaiming her love for another, her supervising professor, an English fop named Robin of all things, whom I had suspected of being gay. Yet, still I argued, confident that intellectual discussion would bring this problem to a more positive resolution. I argued and I pleaded until she brought the argument to an abrupt end by telling me she and Robin had been lovers for months. Yet, still I argued, confident that intellectual discussion would bring this problem to a more positive resolution. I argued and I pleaded until she brought the argument to a crashing end by telling me she was with him, in our bed, even then, even as we spoke.

"His cum is running down my thigh right now, Douglas! Is that over enough for you, for fuck's sake?"

It was.

My world and I went to pieces. U2 was playing there at the end. I had received their latest for Christmas. I was crashing on the couch of an undergraduate friend and her boyfriend. I wish I could remember his name. He was very good to me. I remember listening to "With Or Without You" over and again and drinking warm vodka from the bottle and dialling the phone just to hear the busy signal.

I remember my friend's boyfriend leaning over me;

"Oh, you fucking idiot, Doug. Who's going to clean up this mess?"

I remember trying to explain to him in eloquent martyred silence that I would be okay, the shiny and jagged pieces all around us were just my heart. It would surely heal. Hearts always healed. Mary would come to mend my heart, I told him. I remember him saying that maybe Mary would come to clean up all the fucking blood too. I remember him yelling to my undergraduate friend;

"Call 911 and watch your feet. There's broken mirror all over the fucking place. I think he's stabbed himself in the stomach. Fucking idiot. He's drunk as a skunk too."

I remember going to some awful, dark, and poison sleep place where there was no rest. Looking back on these events, I don't think I woke again until I heard the late Sandy Williams, late of San Francisco, say;

"I'd like that Douglas. That would be fun."

I remember the late Sandy Williams of San Francisco tracing the scars on my torso with the tips of her icy child fingers and with her tongue and asking me how they came to be.

"Remember how your mother told you never to run with scissors," I had answered, glib, embarrassed, ashamed? "Well, I never listened."

She looked at me for a very long time. I could see my lying in her eyes and it felt like a heart attack, a wound.

"Did it hurt?" she asked.

I could see my lying in her eyes and it felt like a heart attack, a wound.

"Not any more," I said.

She stared at me forever then. I saw my lying in her eyes. I saw her forgiveness. She kissed me then most tenderly the way she did, working each lip, with occasional side trips to my eyes and nose and ears.

"I hate that someone might have hurt you," she said finally. "Would you like to go to sleep for a while?"

I allowed that I would and I did after a time, cushioned on her breasts with her stroking the hair around my ear and my temple with angel fingers and humming some beautiful song I could not place.

*

The law offices of Carruthers and Reid were as rich as their business cards. The offices occupied a carefully restored three-story brownstone on one of San Francisco's twisty, hilly streets that ended at the water's edge. There were oils of old, distinguished, anal retentive looking men on dark panelled walls. There was a beautiful, young Asian receptionist in sheer grey stockings. She made me welcome. She made me comfortable in a long-tabled room full of light. She arranged water for our meeting, sparkling and still both.

Here in San Francisco, here in their own element, they made quite the team, Reid and Carruthers did. Here they had a supporting cast too, a gaggle of young associates, a chorus. While I had heard the broad strokes of Sandy's bequests as they affected my life during the Reid/Carruthers road show stop in my little theatre town, I was to learn that there was much more. Mr. Williams, Gareth (what the hell kind of a name was Gareth?), Gary to his friends, had owned what my new lawyer pack called a holding company. He had taken a substantial inheritance from his father who had received a substantial inheritance from his father who had made his pile in railroads and war around the turn of the century. Gareth's father had multiplied the original pile investing in shipping during another war. Gareth had parlayed that pile into an even more substantial pile in the building and real estate boom in California in the sixties and seventies. My, how the money rolled in. No longer active in the buying and selling of real estate nor actually building anything at the time of his death, Gareth Williams had become the benign overseer of an immense fortune and according to the lawyers had been intent in the years before his death on giving it all away. A million to a symphony here; a new shelter for battered women there; cash for schools and museums and libraries; anonymous money for the unlucky unfortunates of the Bay area about whom he read in the papers. In my mind, I pictured him as a sort of West Coast Bruce Wayne. The picture made me smile.

I left the meeting the owner of a San Francisco house, a New York City penthouse apartment, a 'place' in Barbados, some thirty-seven assorted rental properties, skyscrapers mostly, in the continental United States, fourteen more in Britain, 100,000 (give or take) acres of Nevada ranch, and approximately 173 million dollars in cash, stocks, bonds, and negotiable securities, exact value so difficult to calculate with any exact exactitude mind you, the lawyer chorus sang, due to the vagaries of the market. I had smiled and nodded as if to commiserate. Darn vagaries of the market, they would get you every time. Can't live with 'em, can't shoot 'em. When it looked like the meeting was over I had still not said a word beyond good morning and thank you.

"You'll want to see the house, I suppose? Can't have you living out of a suitcase while you're here."

That was Reid. Reid was suddenly unctuous. Reid had become my best pal. I hated Reid. I wanted to break Reid's cheek bone. He checked his watch.

"Perhaps we could do that now. You don't have anything pressing this morning do you, Jerry? Could you arrange that?"

One look at Jerry and I knew that he had nothing pressing this morning. They both turned to me as if proud of a particularly elegant turn of phrase and smiled the same smile. I gave them the smile back. I wondered what I was paying the two of them and their team. I became angry, petulant.

"After we see the house I want to talk to the cop who shot her," I countered.

(The only female member of the team gasped aloud and I knew she would be off the team before days' end. She had been judged and found wanting. She knew it too. She began to gather up the papers in front of her into coloured folders, staring at the oaken tabletop all the time. Her skin had gone ashen underneath a coat of red. Her name was Barb or something like that. Her hair was pulled back in a bun so tight it was a wonder she could blink her eyes.)

"Sure…. I think we can manage that."

That was Reid again, after a while, looking uncomfortable. He didn't sound too sure.

"Why don't you see if you can set that up for the boardroom this afternoon, Brad?"

Brad was a young black man at the table's end. He nodded. He jotted a note – Cop. Afternoon. Boardroom. – I suppose. He hurried off.

"I want to see the cop at his house."

That was me just being a prick. I was angry. I didn't want this to be easy for anyone. Reid sent another peon to catch up with Brad. The rest of us around the table smiled like the parents at a successful shotgun wedding. Some of us set off for the car. The car was long and quiet and black. The driver's name was Larry.

Larry wore a name badge of hard plastic. We rode in silence. I stared out the window. The house was at the end of an impossibly long driveway at the top of a long, impossibly green hill. San Francisco spread out below us like a mat.

*

So, were we in love do you suppose, Sandy and I? We had spoken of love just that once and carried on without a bump or a murmur. We lived a little life of eating and sex and sleep and the shower and the quiet times in between and the occasional car ride some place to eat and back again. We had seven days together. The parts I had liked best were when we had just finished our sex and were resting and waiting for another round or maybe for sleep and she would curl against me and we would talk. I would tell her of my life and I always told the truth and she would tell me of hers and I suspect she was truthful too. There was no reason not to be. We were the proverbial two ships passing in the night or moored together in the middle of the ocean for a week and a bit if you prefer. We neither saw nor spoke to anyone else for that period, except those who brought us sustenance or drove our car or held some door or knocked gently to bring us clean towels and sheets.

*

So, were we in love do you suppose, Sandy and I? On our last night together, we had a room service dinner sent up and spent the evening in bed, languorous and warm. On the final push of our final congress, as I shot the last of my bolts into her and felt her shiver for the last time, I grew melancholic.

"That's the last time I'll feel that Sandy," I said.

I felt ready to cry. I turned away, suddenly petulant, a child denied. She, ever wise, ever cosmopolitan, held me to her and whispered and cooed to my ear and stroked my flank.

"I ruined this, didn't I, Sandy, just then?"

She, ever wise, ever cosmopolitan, held me to her and whispered and cooed to my ear and stroked my flank.

"You didn't ruin a thing, Douglas," she said as I drifted off. "You couldn't ruin this if you tried."

In the morning she dashed about in order to catch her early flight home. I was to keep the car and driver to get me home. We spoke little but looked at each other a lot, little glances mostly from her, shot from the corner of the eye, longer looks from me. I had less to pack. I had nowhere to go.

I watched her brush her teeth and struggle into her panties. I watched her fold her things so woman effortlessly and pack them away. I watched her check her hair as she walked out the door. I watched her look back to the room as the door swung shut. I watched her favour the doorman with a smile to break my heart. I watched her like I was taking pictures. Like a camera, I was mute.

The driver let her out at the departure gate. She refused my offer of company to the gate. I watched. I took the picture of her luggage loaded on the redcap's wagon. I watched as she turned to me for the final time. She should have been an actress for she did the goodbye so perfectly. Standing at close quarters, she placed one hand palm down over my heart and reached up to cup my cheek with the other. Still not a word. She ran the hand from cheek to lips, catching them a little. I felt some moisture as her fingers slid off the end of my chin. She took that hand with its perfect little fingers and held it to her mouth with a motion not like kissing but more like simple contact. Through it all she held my eyes. I felt like I was about to burst into flame.

"You didn't ruin a thing, Douglas. You made everything better," she whispered and then she turned and was gone, suddenly invisible behind a family of travellers and their baggage, and I was back in the car and the car was back in traffic and before I knew it I was back in front of my old home and back at the restaurant and back to my stool at Bentley's and back to my old life and my old tricks. My life became work and home and Bentley's and cocaine. I shocked the boss by offering to pick up extra shifts. I volunteered for lunches and brunches and blue-hair women tour groups that before I had shunned like the plague. I worked more and drank more and snorted more and slept more. So I was when Carruthers and Reid found me that early morning listening to the Gandharvas so very loud. I never said a word to anyone about Sandy. I took no women.

*

So, were we in love do you suppose, Mary and I? I recovered from my wounds and my heart break and my shameful breakdown and got on with my life such as it was. Back to the world of restaurants; the halls of academe had lost their charm as had books and learning and any conversation much beyond the transparent and the banal. My thesis languished in two increasingly battered file boxes which I carted from place to place but never opened. After Mary, life closed up over me like water. My only regret was the typewriter.

My Master's thesis was to have been a biographical sketch of one Walter Weyl, an economist and intellectual and one of the founders of the seminal and extant New Republic magazine. I had secured some travel money from the department to visit Rutgers University where Weyl's papers were housed. Finished there, I had sought out Weyl's last living relative, an ancient grand-daughter still living in the New York City tenement where she had been born. We took tea, this brittle, genteel lady and I. I asked her questions mostly about her mother, Weyl's daughter, and about familial memories of the great but relatively unknown man himself. She was infinitely charming but of no real use. At one point she brought out a photo album and we went through it knee to knee on a small damask couch in front of the window with the sounds of the city alive all round us. There was one photograph with which I was particularly taken, all scalloped edges like photos used to be, yellowed and curling at the corners. It showed Weyl in his young man prime, perched with one hip on the corner of an old wooden office desk, cigarette in hand (his pseudo-scientific record of his many failed attempts to quit smoking would make an interesting side bar to my thesis) and behind him a typewriter, paper still furled in it straight as if he had been interrupted in mid-thought and mid-keystroke and persuaded to strike a pose for the photographer. I mentioned to her my pleasure and how I would like to copy the picture for my own use. Already I was looking to a mass market publication of my biography of Weyl as my first book and the first stone in the path of my historical career as it led to the Bancroft award and a Pulitzer. The dream was real but indistinct.

"I have it still," she said and I, thinking she was speaking of the photograph, assured her that I would simply have it copied and return it to her unharmed.

"No," she said. "I have the typewriter. I used it all through college and after too."

Sure enough, she had the typewriter from the photo languishing in the dust on a shelf in a bedroom at the back of the apartment.

"Would you like to have it? Would it help you write his story?"

I, who had been salivating and entranced and afraid to even touch this artifact, assured her that it most certainly would. I left with the typewriter in a large carton under my arm and the original photo of a smoking, pensive Weyl in my jacket pocket.

"I'm not long for this world," she had said. "Probably just go in the trash after I'm gone."

I assured her that I would treasure it always and treasure it I had, spending more money than I could afford to have it professionally cleaned and restored to working order and purchasing for it a large glass dome to keep off the dust, an antique once used to cover display cakes in a bake shop window.

When Mary pushed me out of her life and out of my life and on to the street, the typewriter had remained with her. I remember how it sat on a corner table in the living room of the apartment we had shared. I remember how our oh-so-historical friends would comment on it and I remember recounting the story of the little old lady in the New York apartment from whence it came. I had not thought of it in years yet, as I rode in the long, black, and quiet car to see Sandy's house, it sprang to my mind like a thrown axe. I felt a renewed and vicious anger at the manner in which it had been stolen from me. It was an Underwood, manu-factured in 1916 and it sold for $8 dollars retail at the time. It was all black metal and the keys were edged in rings of shiny steel. The black matte finish of the space bar had been worn through in the middle from the bounce and the pressure of Weyl's prolific thumbs.

*

From sheer petulance I made the Reid and Carruthers troupe wait outside while I went into Sandy and Gareth's house in the country at the top of the long hill this first time. I suspected it would be the first and only such visit. I did not want to share whatever it was I would find or experience or lose there.

Heart pounding, nauseous, light-headed, I wandered from gloriously appointed room to gloriously appointed room, touching here, lingering there, standing comatose for random long periods thinking about everything at once and thinking about nothing at all.

The house was museum immaculate. I suspected the house was always museum immaculate. I had been told there was a staff of three. A husband and wife team of chauffeur/butler and cook/housekeeper who lived in a little gatehouse cottage had been retained by Reid and Carruthers in the absence of the owners to keep things up to snuff. There was also a groundskeeper who tended the flowers and lawns and oversaw the greenhouse and the ponds and lived in one large room above the garage. I toured to the music of his clipping something at the rear of the house.

I saved the master bedroom until last. When it could no longer be avoided I discovered a large and pleasant and sunny room. There were his and hers dressing and bath rooms to each side of the sleeping area. I dared not enter Gareth's space. I had cuckolded him and could not compound that sin by pawing through his personal things. Sandy's, I felt safe to enter. I even sat on the embroidered seat of a tiny stool in front of her make up table and fingered the disarray of her toiletries and potions and brushes and sprays and unguents and wondered which she had touched last before she had left for the art show. I touched them all, just a whisper. I tucked into my pocket an earring she had been wearing that first night together with me at the Belmont and fingered it in my pocket like a talisman as I walked, the only thing between me and the vampires, the only thing protecting me from some grievous unspecified harm.

On the way back to the front door and to Larry and the limo, I paused in some little room off the living room and helped myself to a large, room temperature, top-shelf single malt from Gareth's bar. There was a painting there above the fireplace in a living room that looked like it had never been used ever, certainly not for living. A life-sized painting, maybe larger, it showed Sandy sitting on the second stair that led to the bedrooms above. Glass in hand, I turned and saw the stair where she had posed. Standing there between the two I could see the picture and be part of it at the same time. She was posed dressed to the nines in a plain white shift of some shiny, diaphanous material and fancy shoes strappy to mid-calf, hair gathered up and held on the top of her head with a little tiara that seemed to glitter with diamonds. You just knew that she and hubby had been off to somewhere terribly fancy. Yet, even dressed as formally as she was, she had posed sitting on that second stair that led to the bedrooms above like an irreverent teenager, a child even, beautiful face, chin cupped in hands, leaning forward, elbows on knees, legs apart, white dress hanging down to cover her treasures. The expression on her face held me; insouciant, shining with beauty, her eyes sparkling with the humour I so loved, just daring the painter to try to capture the spirits of her. I stared at the picture for the longest time. I remembered her walking from the bathroom after a shower all wrapped in a white, white towel.

"It's about fucking time. A man could starve...." I growled with mock anger at her lassitude.

She gave me one of her smiles as only she could do, her whole face turning into this angel thing that glowed with its own light.

"Watch this," she said.

She shrugged off the towel and posed with her breasts just near my face and her hands on my cheeks angling my eyes toward them from a safe distance. I watched as she contrived to make her nipples grow for me. I watched them blossom from the white beds of her breasts like flowers growing in some Walt Disney slow motion.

"That's the most beautiful thing I've ever seen," I said.

"Know how I did that", she asked?

I was awestruck. I was mute.

"I think about making love with you, Douglas, and it just happens."

Glancing down at my tumescence, she whispered;

"Time for my lesson I think."

I assured her it was that time indeed and we were late for dinner. We were always late for dinner.

*

"I want the picture from the mantle," I told the gang back in the car. "That's all. Send it to the Taitinger in Las Vegas care of Mr. King. Sell everything else."

"What about the staff?"

"Give them five years severance and a glowing reference and let them go."

"What about the house?"

"Sell it."

"What should we do with the money?"

"Put it into my checking account."

Fishing a card from my wallet I gave him the bank and branch and account number. 3 or 4 people scratched it down. The car was thick with lawyers.

"For that matter, sell it all. All the buildings and New York and Barbados too. I'll keep the land in Nevada. I might want to live there. I like the desert."

Some lawyer tried to apply the brakes.

"This is highly irregular, Mr. Edgars. We can't have a garage sale like this; we'll lose millions."

"They're my millions," I barked. "Just fucking do it. Sell everything except the painting and the Nevada property. Put all the money in the account I gave you. Give everybody five years pay and send them away."

I was angry about Sandy and about my typewriter and pretty much every other thing. The glass of single malt wasn't helping any. My throat and my guts and my bowels felt like I had swallowed smoke.

Fingering the earring in my pocket, I kept silent as we drove to meet my life's killer. Most of the lawyers pulled out their cell phones and got to murmuring. Larry drove the car. The car was long and quiet and black. The car was pretty much the only thing on the planet I didn't want to punch in the face.

*

The cop's name was Terry Murray and he lived in a cop house with cop pictures on the wall by the front door; Cadet Murray as he graduated the academy, Constable Murray with his arms around his fellow cops in front of a burning, smoking building, Specialist Murray with a scoped rifle posed across his arms, balancing a fancy plaque. A silent, sullen woman let me in and showed me to a little room off the hall, an office of sorts with a desk and a tilty, roll-y chair and two more chairs besides facing the desk for the guests to sit. The cop's wife was a lanky blonde, sadly beautiful in a seventies gone to hell kind of way, busty, leggy, dull hair, grey skin, scared to shit, past her prime. She looked like she was recovering from some wasting tropical disease. She didn't speak as she showed me in and closed the office door on her husband and I with an authoritative slam as if forget we were behind it.

Specialist Murray was sitting behind the desk leaning heavily on it when I entered the room. He came halfway around to shake my hand and, motioning to a bottle on the desk, asked me to join him. The familiar stink of him told me that he had been drunk for a long time. I nodded my assent and we sat on the two chairs facing the empty desk like two truants awaiting the principal if truants were allowed to have tumblers of cheap scotch.

"I was in the army," he began.

"Degree in sociology from Clark State and did ROTC there. Had to, to pay the bills. My dad's dead and there wasn't much insurance. We lived in a trailer, my mom and my two sisters and me. She worked the canning plant. No way I was going to end up at the canning plant. I hated that fucking...."

He paused there for the longest time, time enough to finish his drink and refill and pour a refill for me. I was in no hurry. I let him have his head.

"I grew up with guns," he said. "I could shoot before I could read. My dad taught me how and he was big on safety."

"Never aim it if you can't shoot it," he always said. "If you aim it, shoot to kill it."

He paused again and looked sideways as if to see if I was following the tale and I nodded as if I were.

"That day," he said, "conditions were pretty much perfect. Visibility for miles, no wind; I had a 4 by 4 standing sight picture from a sand bag on top of a patrol car maybe two hundred yards from the kill. At two hundred yards with no wind I could hit a marble off my wife's head 10 times out of 10."

He winced. I looked away to forgive his discomfort.

"You have to understand what it's like to be on that sand bag," he said. He was crying now, crying soundlessly, big tears that I just knew were boiling fever hot rolling from his eyes and off his chin and into his lap. He was a very brave man. He was broken but he was going to finish the job.

"I use a trigger with a break weight of a little over 2 pounds and I'm leaning on it with about a pound and a half and I'm listening in my earpiece for my sergeant to tell me to make the kill. My scope is enough that I can see the blood shot in the mutt's eyes and I'm whispering to the sergeant; "Green One has the kill shot, Green One has the kill shot, Green One has the kill shot;" and the sergeant is whispering back to me "hold, hold, hold", and the bad guy is screaming and dancing and jerking that woman around and back and forth and acting 6 different kinds of crazy and she's just calm, scared sure but going with it all okay and it's hot and I'm sweating and it's like she's starin' right into my scope eye and someone has left a siren on in a car somewhere behind me and it's very loud and I'm tracking that fucker and I am wondering if I have a better shot than my partner and I'm wondering what the fucking hold up is and when are they going to make the call and I know that I am going to love putting the mangey fucker down dead and then the sergeant says out of the blue, "Green One, go with the kill shot" and I squeeze it off and it's a good one and I know I've put it dead centre between his eye and his ear just like we were trained because that's the quickest kill and he'll be in hell before his finger remembers to pull the trigger of his own gun."

Another pause and some silence and we refill our glasses and he leaves to get ice and that necessitates a quick, quiet, frenzied confrontation with the wife which he wins, I suppose, if any man ever wins those, for he is back in his chair and we are drinking cold cheap whiskey and we can't get it down fast enough.

"I never missed like that," he said. "Never in ROTC, never in training, never on the job. I got a fucking medal from the mayor last year for taking out one bad guy from a thousand yards and his friend from even further on the run; put that second shot right in his neck, nearly took his fucking head off."

He brought us over a scrapbook and we leafed through the articles and awards and citations together, knee to knee. I could smell his boozy breath. I found it comforting, familiar, friendly.

"I'm on leave right now, because of the kill," he said, closing the book and putting it to the floor to one side.

"They think I've lost it and they're right. I'm just riding the disability until I can get some sort of pension, you know, off the job for six consecutive months job-related. At least that will leave something for Annie," he nodded to the door that led to his wife.

"I'll probably kill myself after the pension comes through."

He paused again and looked to the door and through it to Annie. He looked to me to see if I were shocked. I wasn't. I was very hard to shock this last little while.

"I'm not much of a husband these days, not much of a man, nothing of a cop. It'll be better for her. She can start again."

We drank a while.

"I still see the sight picture all the time, especially when I try to sleep. Not that I've been sleeping much these days."

He raised his glass in some false toast and I gave it back. Somehow, we had become close.

"I see the kill; skinny Mexican prick, greasy, slicked back hair, sweating up a storm, and I see the pimple on his temple that I'm going to pop for him and I get off the shot and I know it's good and in six tenths of a second he'll be stone cold dead and it feels good and it feels right because he's a bad guy and that's what I do. I kill bad guys with a big gun. But just before I let it go, he jerks his head sudden like he heard a loud noise and his head goes back and hers comes up and the shot hits her in the eye."

He was really crying now.

"Right in the fucking eye. I never missed like that. I still can't believe it. There is no fucking way...."

He snapped his fingers;

"That gets me another medal and a fucking promo-tion and a raise and my picture in the paper."

He snapped his fingers again.

"That gets me a visit from you and sucking the end of my gun."

We made eye contact then for the longest time. I still had not said a word other than a "sure" to his offer of a glass full of scotch. I was having the longest con-versations these days, conversations of great import, all without saying a word.

"Even if I chicken out and don't eat the gun," he said, "I'm going to lose the wife. Sure as shit."

He looked to the door again for a long while. I watched the back of his sweat slick head and smelled the acid smell of him.

"We've been trying to have a kid since our honeymoon. It's what we both want. A family. The doctors say it's her and we can't afford the artificial stuff or adopting so we keep going at it the old-fashioned way."

That last with a smile that me cringe, the way his lips split from his face and his teeth stuck out. He was out of practise. He had forgotten how. He would never smile again.

"That's what I see now when I try to sleep. I see her face in the cross hairs. Gosh, she was a beautiful woman, classy you know. That Mexican mutt with his hands all over her...."

He paused again as if to contemplate the beauty of Sandy in the cross hairs and I let him have his time. I knew his need. I remembered dragging a hotel chair close by the side of our bed as dawn broke and watching her sleep for nearly an hour before she woke and chastised me for my foolishness and gathered me in her arms to let me know that she was flattered and only a bit angry for using her so. We paused together to contemplate the beauty of Sandy and I felt happier than I had in forever just sitting in that little room sharing that thought with him.

"She would have had a beautiful baby. That's what my wife can't get over, the baby, you know, me killing a pregnant woman when we're trying most every night to have one of our own. Can't fault her for that, can you?"

I allowed that I couldn't fault her for that and I wished him good night and thank you and good luck and the same to his wife at the door. The next thing I knew it was two days later and I woke on the floor beside the couch in a suite at the San Francisco hotel, reeking, covered in vomit. The bottles on the floor were legion. The phone was ringing. Somewhere in the recent past I had shit in my pants.

*

Of all the lows to which I had stooped and all the bottoms I had hit, I could not remember a bottom so low as this. Gingerly, shamefully, gagging, I made my way to the bathroom and showered, first with clothes, then without, until finally, when my body was sufficiently clean and my head sufficiently clear, I rinsed the clothes again and left them in a heap at the bottom of the tub and stirred my finger around the tub drain, breaking up the clods of shit into pieces small enough to fit through the opening, all the while gagging and retching and finally dry heaving, oppressed by the smell of me and disgusted by my very existence.

At least most of the shit had been liquid. A census of the debris of the room showed clearly enough that my diet had been largely liquid; gin to begin as was my wont, vodka until it was gone, some scotch, wine of course and beer for when I couldn't decide what next. The mini-bar was a ruin and at some point I had ordered champagne from room service for there were two magnums of fine French in the midst of the debris, one upside down in its wine bucket home and one askance near the pillows of the bed. At several points in the melee I apparently had ordered dinner; a lobster with all the trimmings, drawn butter congealed in a dish and finely halved lemons in a pretty design gone soft, a cheeseburger, one bite gone, a forlorn, untouched Reuben sandwich with fries.

I dressed leaving the fouled clothing in the tub and pushed my remaining belongings into my fine new bag. Then, down to the front desk to arrange a new suite and press into the palm of the surprised clerk there a half inch of hundreds to distribute to the cleaning staff who would have to repair my drunken damage. Back in my new rooms, same as the old rooms but on the other side of the hall, I went to the mini-bar and chugged a beer which I promptly puked up into the bathroom sink in a rush of foam and bile. Then to bed.

I slept long but hard, my slumber disrupted by horrible dreams and waking visions. Witches chased Sandy and I wanting to dismember our baby for some nefarious purpose; Mia Farrow from that movie, you know the one, and George C. Scott from the other, and the witch of the West or the East, whichever one was most wicked; Jack Nicholson from The Shining banging on our door and me throwing my body over Sandy's to protect the two of them. Sometimes in moments of the purest clarity, awake or perhaps asleep, I was with Sandy again, living our idyllic existence of sex and food and drink and I smelt her and tasted her and felt her in my arms and then again, the witches would come. I was having the D.T.'s or perhaps I was going insane or perhaps I had already arrived. I slept as I walked. I walked while I slept. Sometimes I sat on the bed in a huddle of blankets and cried and wailed for the gods to come and get me or the devils or whomever. Someone please, I whined, come for me, for I could no longer stand to be so very alone with my suffering, pathetic self.

*

Slowly lucid, perhaps a day after the fact, I made my way to the suite's little fridge. I sat naked before it and ate the snacks; the M&M's, the macadamia nuts, the Hershey bars. I washed them down with sparkling water until sparkling water and candy came rushing out first one end and then the other and then I was back to the fridge for the crackers and the processed cheese product and the little peppery sausages in a can and more sparkling water until it all stayed down. I slept again huddled in a comforter in the comforting glow and hum of the little fridge. I did not dream or, if I did, I remembered nothing. Remembering nothing was perfect. I had remembered too much.

Three days in, maybe four, I awoke and gulped more of the water and the soft drinks and polished off the chocolate and the cheese. I called Reid and Carruthers and asked them to stop by for a discussion. Turns out I had politely, firmly, and generously bribed the front desk staff upon my return from visiting Murray to make sure I was completely undisturbed. Turns out Reid and Carruthers had been most concerned. Their office had left 60 some messages between them while I lay awash with drink and abed and asleep. I assured them that I had been merely incommunicado while I considered my options. Surely, they understood my need what with the shock of it all. They assured me that they did. I knew that they knew I was lying. They had probably bribed some hotel staff of their own. I knew too that they would never call me on it. I was learning well the rights and privileges of the very rich. I didn't give a shit what they thought.

I asked them how the sale of all my stuff was going and they asked me to call my bank manager most urgently. He was questioning the deposits and threatening to call the police.

I asked how the sale of the house was going and they begged me to reconsider. I asked them to proceed with all possible haste.

I asked them to arrange for Murray and his wife to go on a long ocean cruise at my expense and upon their return to be given the best treatment by the best in vitro fertilization specialists in the city with a bonus of five million dollars to the doctor when they delivered of a healthy baby. They asked me if I wanted to see a doctor myself perhaps for I looked a fright. Had I lost weight? Perhaps I needed some sun. By doctor I could see they meant someone who specialized in affairs of the mind. I assured them that my troubles were those of the heart and thus untreatable with anything but forbearance and time.

I asked them to provide the name of a competent and close-mouthed private investigator who could be trusted to be ruthless and thorough and discreet. They asked if I had any family or friends they could call to help me through this difficult time.

I asked them if they knew of any other lawyers in San Francisco who might honour a client's requests and shut their fucking mouths and they bowed and scraped their way to the door and out.

Alone, I ordered and consumed a small room service meal and fell asleep again, dreamless, in front of some television movie with David Niven and one of the Deborahs with all of the lights on. When I awoke I felt as refreshed as ever I had. I felt strong and self-satisfied, light of heart, resolute of purpose. As I look back on it now I realize I was completely off my millionaire rocker.

*

"I'm not right, down there, for children," she said to me on that first night. Yet she had been right, down there, for everything else. I could smell her still and taste her and feel her supple muscles clench me like a warm, strong, and gentle hand. We had proceeded without precautions. We had proceeded with abandon. I hadn't given the matter a second thought. I sat in my hotel suite in San Francisco. I remembered all of those things and more. I let my anger build.

I listened to music a lot, music from my past exclusively. I had developed a symbiotic telephone relationship with a pimply clerk from a record store down on Market. He brought me stacks of vinyl and talked music with me in exchange for handfuls of hundreds. I had a surplus and thought to use them to buy my peace of mind.

I kept eating regular meals at somewhat regular

times. I kept my drinking to the minimum required for maintenance with a little extra helping at night to help me sleep. I used no drugs. I listened to classical music and classic rock. I read the Romantics; Coleridge and Keats and Wordsworth and that crowd, nothing at all modern. I re-read the Bible from my new perspective. I talked with Reid and/or Carruthers or some member of their staff daily. I phoned my friends back at home and made excuses for my absence. I could not bear to tell them the truth. I called my employer and talked myself out of my job. I called Mr. King back in Las Vegas and assured him I was well and would visit him as soon as my affairs were in order. He knew my lies in a moment but said nothing. I called Specialist Murray and told him no hard feelings and wished he and his wife God-speed on the cruise and best wishes on the fertilization. His wife cried on the phone. I had little hope their marriage would survive. I watched random bits of television. I gave Mary's name to the private investigator suggested by my legal help. I told him to hurry with his report for I had miles to go before I slept. The PI did not seem to recognize the literary reference. Shame that, for I could have given him another and a better. I could have given him some of Byron's *'Siege of Corinth'*. I could have given him;

> *"They did not know how hate can burn,*
> *In hearts once changed from soft to stern;*
> *Nor all the false and fatal zeal*
> *The convert of revenge can feel."*

I could have given him 'I'm not right, down there,

for children' but that one I kept to myself. It burned in me like a coal, like a spark in my eye. It was my last thought before I slept at night and my first thought upon awakening. It was in the hiss of my every breath. It was in the rushing of the blood through my veins. Like my shadow, it was always with me and, even in the brightest of sunshine, it was dark, dark.

*

Subject, Mary ***** is currently employed as a fully tenured Professor of Women's Studies at ***** ***** University.

Subject resides at 124 Birch St. in *****, *****. She is sole owner and occupant of the property. There is no evidence that subject has pets. Appraised value of the property is $425,000. It was purchased in 19** with a cash down payment of $10,000 and currently carries a mortgage of $930 per month. Mortgage will be cleared in 20**.

Subject has no current financial difficulties or en- tanglements. The subject does not own a car. Credit card activity indicates that subject will rent a car as required.

Subject's driving license is current. Subject has three recorded traffic offences; speeding – fine of $118 - May 19** - DUI - license suspended one year – De- cember 19** - DUI - license suspended five years - Jan. 19**. Subject has had no traffic offences since above date.

Subject has been employed at ***** University for 12 years. Subject was previously employed as Assistant Professor of History at ***** University - 19** to 19**. Subject is holder of 3 degrees; B.A. - ***** University - 19** - M.A. - ***** University - 19** - Ph.D. - University of ***** ***** - 19**. Subject was awarded Lawson Prize for Excellence in Historical Research at University of ***** ***** upon graduation.

Subject currently teaches 4 courses at; Introduction to Women in History, Introduction to History of Medicine, Historiography of Women, and The Sexuality of Contemporary History. Subject's courses are consistently over-subscribed. Interviews with subject's students and colleagues are overwhelmingly positive. Subject teaching rating as voted annually by undergraduate students is consistently 'Good' to 'Excellent'. Subject was winner of O'Connor Prize for Excellence in Teaching in 19** and again in 20**.

Subject is active in University governance. Subject serves on the University Senate as a Faculty Representative. She is also one of the current Faculty Representatives on the University's Board of Governors. Subject also sits on the University's Board of Academic Discipline.

Subject has served 4 terms as Contributing Editor of *The Journal of Women's Studies* and is expected to be selected as the next General Editor of said journal.

Subject enjoys preferred reviewer relationships with *Atlantic Monthly*, the *New York Times Review of Books*, the *Los Angeles Times*, and *National Review* and is a regular contributor to said journals.

Subject is regular correspondent for ***** television network on contemporary political issues particularly as they pertain to women.

Subject was winner of the Randolph Award for History in 20** and spent the award year in London, England. She is expected to publish *The History of Bedlam - A Woman's Perspective* in 20**. Publication coincides with subject's next scheduled sabbatical and subject's publisher has begun planning a related lecture tour.

Subject is financial supporter of and/or has lent her name for endorsement purposes to the following organizations.

> University of **** Renewal Campaign
> Save the Whales Foundation (International)
> Society for Women's Education
> Union for Civil Liberties
> Reproductive Rights Organization
> The **** Party of America
> AIDS Ends Now
> National Rain Forest Preservation Society

and several other local or regional organizations of a liberal/left-of-liberal or environmental bent.

Subject has been approached by representatives of the ***** party as a potential national candidate. All such overtures have been turned down.

Subject is currently unmarried and has no recorded children.

Subject health records are clear - no extended hospital stays and no unexplained financial outlays. Subject's most recent physical examination indicates no serious health issues. Subject does suffer from hypertension for which diet and exercise have been prescribed. Subject takes no prescribed medication. Subject does not smoke nor drink.

Subject does not appear to have any current romantic or sexual relationships. Record search indicates a previous marriage - 19** - divorce - 19** - to one Robin *****. Ex-husband is currently Brown Professor of Social History at University of *****. There appears to be no regular correspondence between subject and ex-husband. No financial relationship can be established.

Credit card examination indicates no unusual activity, past or present.

Subject has no travel scheduled for the next four-month period. Subject is scheduled as key-note speaker at the Annual Conference of Women in History in ***** in March of 20**.

Subject is a regular attendee of Tuesday and Thursday morning meetings of Alcoholics Anonymous at Our Lady of Mercy Church at 45 Cedar St. in *****. Subject has been attending meetings as above for 4 years.

Subject parents are deceased - Father - ***** - 19** - Mother - ***** - 19**. Subject's only sibling - **** - born - 19** - currently living in long-term homosexual union in *****. There has been no recent recorded contact between subject and sibling.

Subject CV as filed with university records no siblings extant.

Subject CV as filed with university records no previous marriage.

Appendix A: Financial - Taxation
Appendix B: Social
Appendix C: Marital - Sexual
Appendix D: Academic - Professional
Appendix E: Political
Appendix F: CV - as published
Appendix G: CV - actual

*

So, did I mean to murder Mary as I sat reading and re-reading the private investigator's report. My thoughts were surely those of revenge. She had stolen the life that I was to have had.

The detective had managed a long-distance picture of Mary for me, stolen, off the cuff. There she stood, smiling in conversation with an unknown, mostly unseen woman. She was leaning on a tree wearing an old sweater I thought I remembered as mine. Her teeth were as bad as ever, her skin still blotched. Mary had never been pretty. She wasn't much better now. She was older. Her skin was darker, tighter around the eyes. She was skinny as a rail. She wore her hair short like a man.

As removed as I was, as angry as I was, I felt still a little something of love for her. I felt it tug at my heart and my resolve was, for a moment, gone. I remembered her late-night appearance at my apartment above the garage, scorching hot in the summer. I remembered the landlord's terrorist of a dog that you had to dodge to gain the door. I remembered the way the summer thunder made the roof beams shake and the lights flicker and spark. When she came to me that night it was early in our life together. She was still married. When she came to me that night I still smelled of her; we had fucked goodbye in the front seat of her Volkswagen, me in the passenger seat, her astride me facing front, my hands crushing her little cone tits, urging her further, deeper, her hands clutching the dashboard and pushing back into me.

"Shit! What happened? Come in," I said.

"Thank you," she said. She wasn't even crying.

I took in her bruised face and bloody nose. I took her soaking coat. I hung it across the back of a kitchen chair. I ushered her into my bed-sitting room, laid her down on the bed, and pulled her to me. I loved her mightily right then at that time. We lay for a long-time unspeaking, me trying to pour love into her shivering little frame. We lay at the end of the bed for some hours. After a while we fell to sleep.

"Can I stay with you?" she asked in the morning after the sex and the shower and during the breakfast.

"Of course, you can stay with me, that's the way it was meant to be," I answered.

I really believed that to be true. I really believed that she was how I was meant to be. What else could I say to this woman who I loved mightily, this woman who was wearing my underwear in lieu of hers, wet from my shower, full of my semen, full of my breakfast? So, we began.

*

I sat and studied that stolen picture of Mary for the longest time. I allowed it to fill me, to control me. I thought of Dante. I thought of how he spoke of hypocrites in his eighth ring of Hell.

A painted people there below we found,
Who went about with footsteps very slow,
Weeping and in their semblance tired and vanquished.

They had on mantles with the hoods low down
Before their eyes, and fashioned of the cut
That in Cologne they for the monks are made.

Without, they gilded are so that it dazzles;
But inwardly all leaden and so heavy.

I thought of Dante. I had a weird cross-cultural experience with Dante on an acid-filled evening some years ago. I had translated his Italian to my English. We had drunk to our success at Sunny Jim's Diner down the street from my apartment. We drank until the police came and there was only one of us there to take the heat. It was all the fault of some Italian coward I had explained at the time. The police weren't buying it. My friend Decio had vouched for me down at the station and taken me home to recover. This was when he was still alive.

"What were you thinking, Douglas, what fucked you up this time?" he had asked. "What was it? Some woman?"

I had laughed it off. No mere woman could make me shame myself in Decio's eyes. I had laughed it off until those so many years later when it occurred to me that Des had been right but right some years too early.

It had been some woman that had fucked me up that night and every other night besides. Des had never met her. He had been long dead, wasted by AIDS, by Mary's time.

I was angry with that woman now and more. I was livid for Decio and livid for my Aunt Marie and for my mom and dad and for the way my life had turned out. Mine were the prizes; mine were the plaudits; mine was the little house and the office lined with books; mine the word processor waiting for my words to process; mine was Sandy and the baby. I was angry with Mary for having the strength to finish her thesis and move on when I had abandoned mine and surrendered. I was angry that she had a career. I was angry for the way she had always been able to humiliate me and for the way she had forced me to humiliate myself. I hated her for the way I was drinking and the way I felt in the morning and the way that feeling made me want to drink more and more and never stop. I hated her for the way the drinks tasted good. I hated her because they made me spit and gag and choke. I was mad at her for killing Sandy and killing the baby who I thought had to be mine and killing Sandy's husband. I looked at my reflection in the mirror and I hated her for the swell of my belly and the droop of my buttocks. I hated her for the deterioration of my brain and the fact that I had not put pen to paper with anything but my signature on a credit card slip or a loan agreement or a cheque in so many years. I imagined in my anger and my madness that revenge would be sweet.

"Something of vengeance I had tasted for the first time; as aromatic wine it seemed, on swallowing, warm and racy: its after-flavor, metallic and corroding, gave me a sensation as if I had been poisoned."

That was a Bronte, Charlotte I think. No matter. The facts remained the same. I came to believe.

*

So, did I mean to murder Mary when I sat in my hotel suite in San Francisco and dictated instructions to the private detectives. I had them running all through my life now. I had them finding some and fixing others. I had them trying to make a lifetime of wrong things right.

Find Betty, I said, and find her they did; divorced from her drunken prick of a Lithuanian husband, the bigot, the bastard, the one who beat her and starved her and punished her when I made her work late.

Find Maureen, I said, and find her they did; living in that same little townhouse with her son, the blind one. Her other children, Leo and Deirdre, the beautiful one who would not let me touch her were gone.

Find Bob Hunter, I said, and find him they did; waiting tables in a dreary old-man steak house near the stadium, making good money and pissing it away as he always had. I wondered which busboys he had found to seduce and with whom he was walking the golf course these days.

So it went for some weeks and months. I would wake and sleep at the same times. I would pick up the phone and ask the impossible of persons for whom anything was possible at the price I was willing to pay.

Find my enemies. Find my friends. Report back to me.

Find Davide Carmine, find Tim, find Kim who introduced me to AC/DC, find Snarf who liked the Monkees and played darts so well.

Find George whose parents kept rabbits for eating.

Find Dan Duffy, the holy roller.

Find Smart Kevin and Dom and Josh, find Sally and Moira and Katherine and Bill and Sal and Tony and Jim and his brother and his son. Find them all for me. I have lost touch with everything in the worst of ways.

Find the women, the one-night stands, the ones I loved, the ones that loved me, the ones I never really met. Bring me their stories in your stilted short-form detective language. Bring me their pictures, stolen from a great distance.

Those I had hated brought me new joy as I read of their misfortune. Neil was in prison. Robb's wife was cheating on him with the teenage boy next door. I laughed at the stolen sound of her screaming that boy's name in my stereo speakers.

Those I had loved I reached out to without a word. I bought a new house for Betty, whose roof was beginning to leak. I bought a new car for Rita whose old Nova had finally given up the ghost. I made my amends and worked my remedies for all the others. I had 637 million dollars in my chequing account and nothing to save for. I gave it away like a profligate and then I gave away some more. I gave my lawyers fits. I laughed at them and then I gave some more.

I hired a lawyer I saw on late night television and a notary public from the yellow pages and had them to my hotel to write my will. I lost confidence in Reid and Carruthers and their crowd. As soon as the real estate was sold, I moved my business to a comb-over chartered accountant who had given me his card in the lobby bar.

Always I had the investigators on Mary. I wanted to know her every action and hear her every word. She had become my *raison d'etre*. Just as some years ago she had urged and encouraged and whipped me to work on the venerable Mr. Weyl, so now she spurred me to the reparation of my life. I was the golfer in the sand trap. The ball had been struck. I was earnest, intent on erasing the foot steps, the marks of the club and the ball and the spikes, raking back and forth until it would be as if I had not been there at all. There it was, the dry sand of the future and the wet sand of the past. No matter, for soon it would all be mixed as one, all dried smooth in the sun of the present.

Always I asked them to keep their eye on Mary. I wanted to know every breath she drew and for that privilege I paid through the nose. When I slept I felt her skinny frame beside me. When I ate she sat across from me. When I masturbated she wrenched me from my fantasies and filled my mind with unholy visions and made me come.

I sat in my chair with my knees to my chest wrapped in that thick and rich hotel robe. I slept and I drank and I ate. Sometimes I wept. Sometimes I watched television. Sometimes I listened to music. Sometimes I laughed Sometimes I howled at the moon like a mad dog. It was all one and the same.

*

So, did I mean to murder Mary when I showed up at her door that night? I had covered my tracks well. One story for the lawyers and hotel keepers in San Francisco and another for Las Vegas. To each I was to be in the other place while I was in neither. I was in the driver's seat of a paid-for-in-cash, new-to-me car and in another car just like it and then I was knocking at Mary's front door, sweating, freezing, trembling like a prom date.

She swung the door open wide and fast. She wore a sour expression as if she had been expecting someone to whom she could give some serious shit. She was obviously perplexed to see an unfamiliar, innocent face. I was wearing the best smile that I could muster. I broke the silence.

"It's me, Mary. It's Douglas. Don't you remember?"

After a longish while she did. I saw her face change from angry to perplexed to confused to understanding and back to confusion and resigned acceptance. Somewhere in there she ushered me inside.

"It's been a long time, Douglas. Did you just happen to be passing by, in the neighbourhood, as it were? I don't recall you ever having my address."

"I didn't," I said, "but you're famous these days. I heard you on NPR the other day talking about something or another. Hearing you brought back a lot of memories. I'm in town for a bit and I thought...."

I left all that just hanging and gave her another of my most friendly of smiles, the false one that I had learned young in the diner and perfected with various women. I felt it like to rip the muscles in my throat.

She looked at me seriously then. I recognized her suspicious look, her 'if you're fucking with me, you'll be sorry' look. I watched it morph into her deadly 'you hurt me, I hurt you worse' look. I surrendered another of my most benign smiles.

"How have you been," I asked?

Soft. Innocent. Lamb got nothing on me.

The transformation took her then. I saw her turn from the suspicious young professional who had opened her door to a situation she had been expecting to control, even dominate, turn into the feral cat cornered in the alley and worried for its life, turn into the polished professional, the politician academic, back on her feet, facing just another cocktail-party-uncomfortable situation that could and would be survived, outlasted, laughed about later with her smart academic friends over drinks and appies. I saw her eyes flash with pity and hatred and fear and anger and confusion, but no apology, not a hint of remorse. I saw her eyes fill with 'once more into the breach' and I was in.

"I've only got a few minutes, Doug. I've got a thing tonight. If you had called ahead...."

We both let it hang.

She was dressed in leggings and a tee and trainers. She looked about as far from having a thing tonight as it was possible to get.

"You're looking well," she said.

We both knew that was a lie. I looked like well-dressed shit. We let it go.

"So are you," I said.

We both knew that was a lie. She looked like fear and resignation. We let it go.

She moved to take me in her arms. I let her and took her in mine. We hugged for a beat. With a rush I recognized the earth smell of her hair and felt my resolve weaken. I associated the smell of her with orgasm and sweat and pleasure and strong emotion. I pushed her away as if to get a better look.

"The years have been kind," I said.

We both knew that was a lie. She was leaner and meaner, strong and wiry. She looked like a spring. She had a hunted look about her too and a yellowish cast to the skin across her cheeks. I wondered if she had been sick.

"Can I get you something," she asked? "I'm not drinking these days but I seem to remember that you liked a good belt or three every now and then. I think I have some decent sherry."

She chuckled. She smiled as if we were sharing a tender moment.

I chuckled. I smiled as if we were sharing a tender moment.

In my heart, I was shrieking;

"I never really drank until I met you, you fucking harridan! I never really drank until you crushed my heart under your heel and now I can't seem to drink enough. I'm always dry. I'm always thirsty."

I felt my anger build within me. I felt its sweetness start to fill me and pump me bigger. I smiled as if we were sharing a special moment.

"Some water would be good. I really can't stay long."

I let her off the hook. I saw her shoulders sag with relief as we moved toward the kitchen. On the dining room table, I saw the typewriter, my Weyl typewriter. It was sitting there in the centre of the table on a lace doily thing, no glass cover now, some dried flowers stuck here and there in the keys to make it into a centre piece.

"That's nice," I said, pointing it out. "Distinctive. Different."

"Oh that. The typewriter," she said. "I found it in a flea market or something, I think. Years ago. Campy huh? It used to have a glass dome over it but it got broken at a party."

I found myself in a frenzy and a calm and a fury all at once.

"Yeah, a real conversation piece," I said out loud.

In my brain I was shrieking as I remembered Weyl's aunt passing the torch to me.

"I'm not long for this world," she had said. "Probably just go to the trash after I'm gone."

Here I saw it as much as in the trash, worse even, unappreciated, my typewriter, the typewriter on which Weyl had written in 1912;

Our country..."today is in a sombre, soul-questioning mood. We are in a period of clamor, of bewilderment, of an almost tremulous unrest."

I had planned to call my thesis "*An Almost Tremulous Unrest*" and that thesis was to bring me fame and fortune and responsibility and a sense of purpose. It was to make my life not empty but full. I remembered the original report of Weyl's death and how the policeman on the scene had recorded that '...subject's head is resting on typewriter keys covered with sputum'. Weyl had died in the postwar Spanish Flu pandemic. He had choked and strangled on his own mucus. I envied him that awful death in his New York apartment so long ago.

As she moved before me talking all animated now about her upcoming address to some society and was I still in the history field and had I read her books and how she had almost dedicated one to me but didn't know if I would understand and how she had looked for me to explain and make amends. Her words were all a jumble. She was all a jumble. She moved before me through the dining room. I saw her open the cupboard for a glass and turn and bend to the sink tap for water. I was filled with an unfathomable fury. I raised up the typewriter in both hands. I rushed at her, two steps maybe, with it suspended above me. I brought it crashing down onto the back of her skull. I felt it cut and break and bite into her with the satisfying slap of pounded meat. I forced her body against the counter with my weight. Her head flopped to the sink. The typewriter was tough to pull from her skull. I hit her again. Maybe I hit her again or again. I forced her body against the counter with my weight. Her head bled terribly into the sink. With a wrenching, sicking sound I pulled the typewriter from her skull and allowed her to slump to the floor. Her brains were spread across the back of her and the blood was still so much everywhere that I had to step back to avoid being caught in its rush.

*

I was at the front door of the Taitinger with Mr. King welcoming me home. Oscar, the bell captain, was reaching for my bag with the typewriter stuffed safely inside. I was at the mini-bar of my old suite offering Mr. King a drink and he was accepting and he was asking if I were going to stick around for a while. Through it all I felt pretty much normal, more so than in a long while. We sighed together and sat in a comfortable silence. The twin sighs said we had both had quite a day.

"Get everything pretty much sorted then, did you, while you were away," he asked after a while.

"Pretty much," I said. "I needed to get away for a bit, clear my head like, figure some shit out."

We paused and sipped and smoked for a bit and kept our silence for we had become comfortable with that.

"I'm going to quit drinking," I said. "Going to quit

the dope too. I'm getting tired of waking up tired you know."

"I think that's a fine idea," he said. "I can help you with that if you want. I've been there. Still am. Always will be."

We paused and sipped and smoked for a bit and kept our silence for we had become comfortable with that.

"I think I'm going to move out of the hotel, out into the desert," I said. "I apparently own a shit-ton of land out there somewhere. I'd going to build a house and a barn and get some animals. Not cows though. Cows scare me. Horses maybe. Rhinos maybe. I've always loved rhinos. Hippos too. A couple of giraffes too maybe. Probably get a bunch of cowboys to help me run things. You know any cowboys?"

"I think that's a fine idea," he said. "Horses and rhinos and hippos and giraffes are among the finest of the animals. Alas, I don't know any cowboys but I'll make a couple of calls."

We paused and sipped and smoked for a bit and kept our silence for we had become comfortable with that.

"I'm going open up a restaurant, on the strip probably. I'm going to call it 'Sandy's'."

"I think that's a fine idea," he said.

He sparked another cigarette and offered one to me.

"Las Vegas can always use another fine restaurant," he said.

We paused and sipped and smoked for a bit and kept our silence for we had become comfortable with that.

"That painting I've been keeping for you would look fine in the entryway or maybe above the bar," he said.

"I was thinking above the bar."

"That's Sandy is it, that painting," he asked?

I nodded. He smiled.

"You weren't lying. Beautiful woman," he said. "Special beautiful."

We paused there a moment to contemplate Sandy's special beauty.

"Will you come and run it for me, Mr. King?"

He looked at me for a long while.

"No, I don't think I could, even if I wanted to. It's not my restaurant. I don't think it will be that kind of restaurant at all. Besides, I have my hotel to run." he said finally. "I'll visit often though. I think it will become my favourite place, other than the Taitinger, that is."

He smiled and we were fine again.

I said that I had expected as much and hoped that it would be so.

We raised our glasses.

"To Sandy's," he said.

We clinked and we drank and refilled.

"To Sandy," I said.

We clinked and we drank and refilled

We moved on to other things.

We were fine.

The End

www.ingramcontent.com/pod-product-compliance
Lightning Source LLC
Chambersburg PA
CBHW020632180626
46816CB00003B/933